Manipulation:
The Curse of Kisses

Arjun Pitcher

Preface

In our lives, we often believe we have control over our desires, our connections, and the relationships we nurture. But what happens when that control is wrested away? What happens when the very essence of who we are is twisted by forces beyond our comprehension?

Manipulation: The Curse of Kisses explores this unsettling journey through the life of Nisha, a young woman who dares to seek change but finds herself ensnared in a web of unintended consequences. It is a story about power, vulnerability, and the dangerous allure of desires both our own and those imposed upon us.

This book is not just about Nisha's struggles—it is a reflection on the human condition, the boundaries of consent, and the ways in which external forces can influence our lives. It delves into themes of identity, manipulation, seduction, mind control, influence, submission, self-discovery, and resilience, asking readers to consider where personal agency ends and manipulation begins.

As I wrote Nisha's story, I found myself questioning the lines between right and wrong, love and obsession, and freedom and control in an erotic way. I hope that as you immerse yourself in Nisha's world, you will find moments that resonate with your own experiences and leave you pondering the complexities of human emotions and relationships.

This book is not merely a journey—it's an exploration. And as Nisha's story unfolds, I invite you to think about your own boundaries, desires, and the forces that shape who you are.

Thank you for stepping into this world with Nisha. May her story leave an impression, and may her courage inspire your own.

— *Arjun Pitcher*

Table of Content

Chapter – 1 The Trap

The day was cool and overcast as Nisha stepped out of her college, the soft whispers of an impending storm brushing against her senses. The bustling chatter of her classmates faded into the background as she adjusted the strap of her satchel and walked purposefully towards the edge of town. Her destination loomed in her thoughts—a secluded cottage at the end of a winding dirt road, known to the locals as the home of Vashika, the enigmatic crystal ball reader.

Nisha's curiosity had been piqued by whispers among her friends. Tales of Vashika's uncanny accuracy and otherworldly demeanor were enough to draw her in. A small thrill of nervous anticipation coursed through her. She didn't entirely believe in the supernatural, but something about Vashika's reputation had captivated her.

The air grew heavier as Nisha approached the cottage. Wildflowers swayed along the path, their vibrant colors muted in the growing dusk. The cottage itself was as peculiar as its owner—dark wood panels, creeping ivy, and a faint glow from the windows gave it an otherworldly allure. Nisha hesitated at the door, her heart thudding in her chest.

She knocked lightly. The sound was immediately swallowed by the thick silence surrounding the cottage.

The door creaked open, revealing Vashika herself. She was striking—tall and elegant, with flowing raven-black hair, and eyes like shards of onyx. She wore a deep burgundy dress adorned with intricate silver embroidery, giving her the air of someone both ancient and timeless.

"You've come," Vashika said softly, her voice like a velvet caress. Her lips curled into a knowing smile. "I was expecting you, Nisha."

Nisha blinked in surprise. "You know my name?"

Vashika chuckled lightly. "The crystal ball knows many things. But please, come in. Let us discover what the fates have in store for you."

Nisha stepped inside, feeling an odd mix of trepidation and excitement. The room was dimly lit, the walls lined with shelves of peculiar objects—bottles filled with mysterious liquids, bundles of dried herbs, and ancient tomes. At the center of the room was a small round table, draped with a black velvet cloth. Upon it sat the crystal ball, shimmering faintly as though it held a secret light.

"Sit," Vashika instructed, gesturing to a chair opposite her own. Nisha complied, her pulse quickening.

Vashika took her seat, her fingers hovering over the crystal ball. "Are you ready to see what lies ahead?"

Nisha nodded, her voice barely a whisper.
"Yes."

Nisha adjusted herself in the chair, smoothing her white top and blue skirt nervously. Due to which the strap of her black bra was visible to Vashika. Vashika looked at it with a mysterious smile and bite her lips. The room's heavy, perfumed air seemed to cling to her skin, making her hyper-aware of every move she made. She leaned forward slightly, feeling the weight of Vashika's gaze as she fiddled with the edge of her pink-painted nails.

Clearing her throat softly, she finally spoke, her voice a mixture of curiosity and caution. "Do you really… see the future? Can you actually tell me what's going to happen?"

Vashika's dark eyes seemed to glint with hidden knowledge. A faint smile played at her lips as she leaned forward, her hands gliding over the smooth, radiant surface of the crystal ball.

"Not only can I see it, dear Nisha, but I can help you understand it," she said, her voice a hushed murmur that sent a shiver down Nisha's spine. "The threads of fate are delicate, but with the right guidance, they can be woven into something extraordinary."

The glow of the crystal ball brightened as Vashika moved her hands, light and shadow playing across her elegant fingers. Her gaze never left Nisha's face, as though she were searching for something within her.

"What is it you wish to know first?" Vashika prompted, her tone inviting yet laced with a mysterious gravity.

Nisha hesitated, biting her lip slightly before deciding on her first question. She steadied herself and spoke.

"What does my future hold? Will I… achieve something great, or is there something I should be prepared for?"

Vashika's smile deepened, her eyes glinting as though she had been waiting for just that question.

Vashika let out a soft chuckle, the sound like a melody laced with secrets. She ran her fingers delicately over the crystal ball, her long nails clicking faintly against the surface. The glow within the orb pulsed, shimmering with colors that seemed to shift and dance like a living thing.

"You, my dear, are destined for greatness," Vashika said, her voice resonating with a hypnotic cadence. Her eyes locked onto Nisha's, deep and unreadable. "The future ahead of you is filled with triumph, admiration, and influence. You will achieve things that many can only dream of."

Nisha blinked, leaning forward in her seat. Her heart fluttered at the words, a mix of excitement and disbelief rising within her. "Really?" she asked softly. "What kind of greatness? I mean... how do you know?"

Vashika smiled again, enigmatic and knowing. "The crystal ball reveals it to me. But it is not merely the ball. You possess a certain... energy, Nisha. A rare force that draws the world to you. People will flock to you, entranced by your charm, compelled to follow where you lead. Opportunities will fall at your feet, and you will leave an indelible mark upon this world."

Her voice dropped lower, almost conspiratorial. "But greatness always comes at a cost, my dear. The fates demand balance. As you rise, you must be mindful of the shadows that seek to pull you down."

Nisha felt her throat tighten. The intensity of Vashika's words and the rhythmic glow of the crystal ball had her completely enraptured. She barely noticed the way Vashika's voice seemed to wrap around her thoughts, sinking into the recesses of her mind.

"Embrace this destiny," Vashika continued, her tone softening into something almost tender. "But know that it will require more than ambition. It will require... transformation."

A subtle shiver coursed through Nisha as she tried to process the strange sense of foreboding mixed with promise.

Nisha hesitated, her cheeks flushing slightly as she leaned forward on the table. Her fingers played with the hem of her white top, and her voice came out softly, almost as though she were embarrassed to admit it.

"I… I like someone," she said, her words barely above a whisper. "But he doesn't seem to notice me. I just… I want him to like me back. I want to be someone who can draw people to me, who they can't help but notice."

Vashika's eyes glimmered, the shadows of the room dancing in their depths. She leaned back in her chair, a slow, calculating smile spreading across her lips. "Ah," she said, drawing out the word as though savoring it. "So you wish to become a beacon, someone who can captivate anyone with a mere glance, someone who commands the hearts of others effortlessly."

Nisha nodded, her excitement growing. "Yes. Can you make that happen? Can you help me?"

Vashika tilted her head, her long, dark hair cascading over one shoulder. Her smile deepened, but there was a weight to her expression now, a gravity that made Nisha's breath catch.

"I can," Vashika said simply. "But you must understand what you are asking for, Nisha. This is no simple charm or fleeting spell. To become what you desire, to hold such a power over others, is to open yourself to forces far beyond your control."

Vashika leaned forward, her hands clasped on the table, her voice dropping to a low, hypnotic whisper. "Are you sure you truly want this? Once a spell like this is cast, it cannot be undone. It will change you—and everyone you encounter—forever. It will give you what you desire, yes. But with every gift comes a price."

Nisha blinked, feeling her heart pound faster. "What kind of price?"

Vashika's smile took on a hint of something darker, almost mischievous. "You will draw people to you, irresistibly so. Their hearts, their thoughts, their desires… all will turn to you. But such passion burns hot, and it cannot be contained. They will crave you, Nisha, sometimes to the point of madness. Their need for you will blind them to everything else. Do you understand? This spell will make you a flame in a world full of moths."

Nisha felt a shiver run through her, but at the same time, she couldn't deny the thrill that coursed through her veins. The thought of being desired, admired, and powerful was intoxicating.

Vashika's voice softened, almost coaxing now. "So, I ask again: Are you truly ready to embrace this? To wield the power you seek, knowing it will bring both joy and… chaos?"

The crystal ball flickered faintly, as though waiting for Nisha's answer.

Nisha after giving it a thought had agreed to carry on the spell with Vashika as she was madly falling for this guy.

Vashika ' expression turned resolute as she straightened in her chair. She placed her hands delicately on the crystal ball, her fingers moving in graceful arcs as though drawing invisible threads from the orb. Her voice became low and melodic, each word laced with an eerie energy that seemed to reverberate in the air around them.

"By the forces unseen and the tides of desire,
Let Nisha's spirit burn like fire.
All who gaze upon her shall crave,
Their hearts, their minds, their will enslave.
Irresistible, alluring, a beacon so bright,
She shall command devotion, day and night."

She paused, her dark eyes meeting Nisha's as the glow of the crystal ball grew stronger.

"By the forces unseen and the tides of desire,
Let Nisha's spirit burn like fire…"

Vashika repeated the incantation, her voice now stronger, the air in the room growing heavy with power. A faint, shimmering aura began to form around Nisha, a sensation that prickled at her skin and made her heart race.

"By the forces unseen and the tides of desire,
Let Nisha's spirit burn like fire."

The spell crescendoed, and the room fell eerily silent for a moment, as though the world itself held its breath. Then, with a soft whoosh of air, the light in the crystal ball faded, leaving a faintly pulsing glow that mirrored the wild thrum in Nisha's chest.

Vashika leaned back, a satisfied smile on her face. "It is done," she said softly. "When you leave this room, the spell will take hold. Anyone who lays eyes upon you will find themselves unable to resist your allure. Women, in particular, will be captivated beyond reason—"

"Wait, what?" Nisha interrupted, her brow furrowing in confusion. "Women? No, no, no— I said men! I like men. You're casting the wrong spell!"

Vashika's smile did not falter, but her tone held a calm finality. "Ah, but power isn't so easily tailored," Vashika said with a soft chuckle, her gaze steady. "It flows where it's needed most, not where it's wanted. You'll come to understand this in time. The spell has already been cast, Nisha. Such is the nature of magic—it cannot be reversed once set in motion. You wished to be irresistible, and now you are. You will find the power far exceeds what you imagined. Women will be drawn to you with an intensity that will change your life forever."

Nisha's stomach dropped. She bolted upright from the chair, her voice rising in panic. "No! That's not what I wanted! Fix it—undo it!"

Vashika simply shook her head, her expression serene. "This is what fate has decided for you. I warned you—such power comes with its own will. Now, go. Step into the world and claim your destiny."

Before Nisha could protest further, Vashika gestured towards the door. The spell's energy clung to her like a second skin, pulsing faintly as though waiting for its moment to unleash its full potential. Nisha turned, the weight of the situation sinking in as she opened the door to leave.

"Remember," Vashika called after her, her voice laced with something between warning and encouragement. "Sometimes the greatest blessings are born from the things we least expect."

Nisha with anger steps out of the door thinking what stupidity Vashika has done. Instead of guys now woman will feel attracted towards her. She did not know what to do with this thing.

Chapter – 2 The Woman at the Bus Stop

The cool evening air greeted Nisha as she stepped out of Vashika's cottage, her mind swirling with frustration and disbelief. The faint shimmer of the spell clung to her like an invisible aura, though she couldn't yet sense its effects. She grumbled to herself, her arms crossed tightly as she walked along the narrow dirt path back towards town.

At the edge of the main road, a lone woman stood waiting at a small, weathered bus stop. She was perhaps in her mid-thirties, with wavy chestnut hair that spilled over her shoulders. Her pale blue eyes were framed by faint crow's feet, giving her a mature and approachable air. Her outfit was simple but stylish: a fitted navy blazer over a white blouse, paired with high-waisted beige trousers and low heels. A brown leather satchel hung over one shoulder, completing her professional look.

The woman, whose name was Clara, was a marketing executive on her way home from a long day at work. She was returning to her small apartment downtown, where her partner of six years, Rachel, was waiting for her. Clara and Rachel had been planning a quiet dinner together, something to reconnect after a busy week. But as she stood at the bus stop, checking her watch, her plans for the evening were about to take an unexpected turn.

Spotting Nisha approaching, Clara decided to ask for the time, her phone buried somewhere in her bag. She took a step closer, offering a polite smile. "Excuse me," she said gently, her voice kind and unassuming. "Could you tell me what time it is?"

Nisha glanced at her, momentarily distracted from her inner turmoil. She pulled her phone from her pocket and replied, "It's 7:15."

But as the words left her lips, something shifted in Clara's demeanor. Her polite smile softened into something warmer, almost dazed. Her blue eyes lingered on Nisha's face longer than necessary, her expression changing from casual to captivated. She seemed to forget why she had approached in the first place, her gaze tracing Nisha's features as though she were seeing her for the first time.

Clara took a small step closer, her voice dropping slightly. "Thank you," she murmured, her tone unsteady. Her cheeks flushed faintly, and her fingers tightened around the strap of her satchel. She appeared… drawn in, as though an invisible force tethered her to Nisha's presence. The professional air she carried seemed to melt away, replaced by a vulnerable, almost desperate intensity.

Nisha noticed the sudden change and felt her stomach twist. She had no idea what to do as Clara's polite inquiry morphed into something far more unsettling.

Clara hesitated for a moment, as though struggling to find the right words. Her eyes remained locked on Nisha, and there was a subtle tremor in her voice when she spoke again. "You know," Clara began, her cheeks now a deep shade of pink, "I don't usually… stop to talk to strangers. But there's something about you." She took a step closer, her satchel sliding off her shoulder and landing on the bench beside her. Her hands fidgeted nervously, but her gaze was unwavering.

"I mean, I just… you're really stunning," Clara said, her tone soft but undeniably intense. She laughed nervously, brushing a strand of chestnut hair behind her ear. "I don't know why I'm saying this, but you… you're captivating. I feel like I can't look away."

Nisha froze, her heart thudding against her ribcage. "Uh… thanks?" she replied awkwardly, taking a small step back. Her mind raced. *Is this the spell already? Is it really this powerful?*
Clara smiled, almost shyly, her blush deepening. "I know this sounds crazy, but… would you want to—" She caught herself, her eyes darting down briefly before returning to Nisha's face. "I mean, would you maybe like to grab a coffee? Or something? I don't even know where that came from, but I… I feel like I need to get to know you."

Her voice was tinged with desperation, her professional poise unraveling by the second. She seemed to be battling an internal struggle, aware on some level that her feelings were irrational but unable to resist the pull she felt toward Nisha.

Nisha's pulse quickened as she realized Clara's gaze had dropped briefly, lingering on her lips before darting back to her eyes. The spell's effect was undeniable now, and it was far more intense than she had imagined. Clara's breathing had grown shallow, her presence becoming almost suffocating.

Nisha gave Clara a tight, nervous smile and took another step back, the edge of her discomfort starting to show. "Uh, no thanks," she said quickly, forcing a polite tone. "I've got somewhere I need to be."

Without waiting for Clara's response, she turned on her heel and started walking briskly down the sidewalk, her thoughts a chaotic mess. *This spell is insane. I need to figure out how to deal with this.* But before she could make it far, the sound of footsteps behind her made her heart sink.

"Wait!" Clara called, her tone sharper now, almost commanding. "Don't just walk away from me like that."

Nisha's pace quickened, but Clara easily matched her stride. The soft, kind demeanor Clara had shown earlier was gone, replaced by a focused intensity that bordered on aggressive. Her voice, when she spoke again, was firmer, less apologetic. "Look, I'm trying to talk to you. You don't just blow someone off like that."

"I told you, I'm busy," Nisha said, glancing over her shoulder. Her pulse raced as Clara closed the distance between them.

Clara reached out, grabbing Nisha's arm to stop her. Her grip was firm, and the sudden contact made Nisha's breath hitch. "Don't walk away from me," Clara said, her voice low but insistent. Her other hand moved, brushing against Nisha's shoulder in a way that felt far too familiar. "You feel it too, don't you? This… connection? It's like I can't stop thinking about you, can't stop wanting—"

"Hey, stop!" Nisha snapped, pulling her arm free and stepping back, her voice shaky but firm. She held her hands up defensively, glaring at Clara. "You're crossing a line. Back off."

But Clara wasn't deterred. She stepped closer again, her movements more assertive now, her hand trailing down Nisha's arm in a way that sent a chill up her spine. "You're so beautiful," Clara murmured, her voice dropping to a husky whisper. "I don't even know what's happening to me, but I can't stop. I need to be near you."

Nisha's mind raced as she tried to figure out what to do. The spell's influence had completely overtaken Clara, and it was clear her rational thoughts were slipping away. Panic bubbled in Nisha's chest as Clara moved closer still, her touch lingering, her gaze intense and unrelenting.

Nisha stepped back, her voice trembling but resolute. "Please, just leave me alone," she said, holding up her hands as if to ward Clara off. "I'm only 18, and you—you look like you're in your 30s. This isn't right. Just… let me go."

Clara hesitated for a fraction of a second, her expression flickering with something like guilt or hesitation. But the spell's pull was overpowering, drowning out reason and morality. Her lips parted as if to say something, but instead, she moved closer, her hands reaching out toward Nisha again, her touch brushing against Nisha's wrist.

"Age doesn't matter," Clara murmured, her voice soft but filled with an obsessive intensity. "It's not about that—it's about how I feel when I'm near you. I don't know why, but I can't stop myself. Please, just… stay for a minute."
"Stop it!" Nisha exclaimed, jerking her arm away and backing up further. Her heart pounded, and her pulse felt like it might burst from her chest. She could see the internal conflict in Clara's eyes, but it was clear that whatever rational part of her remained was losing the battle.
Nisha's voice grew stronger, fueled by desperation. "Look, you don't even know me! Whatever you're feeling—it's not real! Just… walk away. Please. I don't want this."

Clara paused, her chest rising and falling heavily as if she were trying to catch her breath. Her hands trembled slightly, and for a moment, it seemed like she might relent. But the spell's influence was relentless, binding her to the overwhelming pull of Nisha's presence.

Nisha's stomach twisted in fear and frustration. *This spell is a nightmare. How do I make it stop?* she thought, glancing around for help or an escape.

Clara's gaze turned molten with a mix of desperation and desire as she closed the distance between herself and Nisha in an instant. Her hands gently but firmly cupped Nisha's face, and before Nisha could fully react, Clara leaned in, her lips pressing against Nisha's in a sudden, overpowering kiss.

Nisha froze, her mind screaming in panic. She instinctively raised her hands to push Clara away, but Clara's strength and determination made it impossible. Nisha's smaller frame was no match for Clara's commanding presence, and despite her efforts to resist, she felt trapped.

"Mmph! Stop!" Nisha tried to protest, her voice muffled against Clara's lips. Her heart pounded wildly as the warmth of Clara's touch overwhelmed her. She twisted her head, trying to break free, but Clara held her steady, her actions fueled by an almost otherworldly compulsion.

The kiss lingered for what felt like an eternity, and when Clara finally pulled back, her expression was dazed, her chest heaving. Her hands still rested on Nisha's shoulders as if she couldn't bear to let go. "I… I don't know what's come over me," Clara whispered, her voice shaky but laced with fervor. "I've never felt anything like this before. You're… intoxicating."

Nisha stumbled back, her cheeks flushed with a mixture of anger and humiliation. "What is wrong with you?" she snapped, her voice trembling. She wiped her mouth with the back of her hand, her breath coming in sharp gasps. "I told you to stop! I didn't want this!"

Clara blinked, a flicker of guilt crossing her face, but it was quickly replaced by the same burning intensity that had overtaken her earlier. "I… I couldn't help it," she said, her voice soft, almost pleading. "You don't understand. It's like… I'm drawn to you, like I don't have a choice."

Nisha took another step back, her mind racing as the weight of the spell's consequences began to sink in. She felt trapped, the lingering sensation of the unwanted kiss a harsh reminder of the power Vashika had unleashed on her.

Nisha's eyes brimmed with tears as she looked at Clara, her voice trembling with emotion. "I've never kissed anyone before," she whispered, her words heavy with a mixture of sadness and anger. She wiped at her cheeks, her breath hitching as the reality of the moment sank in. "I'm only 18, and I thought… I thought my first kiss would be with someone special. With a guy I have a crush on. Not like this. Not you."

Clara's expression faltered, a flicker of awareness cutting through the haze of the spell. For a moment, her hands dropped to her sides, and she took a small step back. The weight of Nisha's words seemed to pierce through the obsession clouding her mind. "I…" Clara began, her voice shaky. "I didn't know. I didn't mean to—"

"You *did* mean to!" Nisha snapped, her voice cracking with pain and anger. "You couldn't stop yourself, could you? Because of this stupid spell! You don't even like me; you don't even know me. It's just… it's not real!"

Clara looked down, her lips parting as though she wanted to say something, but no words came. The guilt and confusion in her expression deepened, yet the compulsion still lingered in her eyes, a faint glint of the spell's power keeping her tethered to Nisha.

Nisha turned away, clutching her arms tightly around herself as if trying to hold herself together. The tears fell freely now, and she didn't bother wiping them away. "You ruined something special for me," she said, her voice quieter but no less pained. "I didn't ask for this. I didn't want this to happen."

The air between them grew heavy with tension, the spell's influence a constant, suffocating presence that Nisha couldn't escape. Clara took another hesitant step forward, her voice soft. "I… I don't know what's happening to me. I'm so sorry, Nisha. I don't know why, but I can't seem to stop… feeling this way."

Nisha didn't look back at her, her fists clenching as her anger warred with the aching vulnerability of the moment. "Just stay away from me," she said, her voice firm despite her tears. "Please. Just go."

Nisha barely had time to process the torrent of emotions swirling within her before Clara stepped closer again, her expression pleading but still tinged with that same, overpowering desire. Nisha held up her hands to stop her, her voice shaky. "No, Clara, I said stop—"
But Clara ignored her, driven by the irresistible compulsion of the spell. Her hands gently but firmly cupped Nisha's face again, her touch softer this time yet no less assertive. "Let me make it right," Clara murmured, her voice heavy with regret and longing. "I ruined something special for you, but... maybe this can be something special too. Let me give you this."

"Clara, no—" Nisha tried to pull away, but Clara leaned in again, her lips pressing against Nisha's in a kiss far deeper and more fervent than the first. Nisha's protests were muffled as Clara held her firmly, tilting her head slightly to deepen the connection. Her hands moved to Nisha's shoulders, holding her in place as the kiss grew more impassioned.

Nisha felt overwhelmed, her smaller frame no match for Clara's strength and determination. She squirmed and tried to push Clara away, but it was as though the older woman couldn't hear her, lost entirely to the spell's pull. The seconds dragged on like an eternity, every moment of the kiss more intense and all-consuming.

Tears slipped from Nisha's eyes, her chest tightening as she struggled against the overpowering force of both Clara's actions and the magic fueling them. *Why is this happening?* she thought, panic surging through her. *Why won't she stop?*

For three long minutes, Clara kissed her, her lips moving with a passionate fervor that only made Nisha feel more helpless and trapped. When Clara finally pulled back, her breath came in shallow gasps, her cheeks flushed, and her eyes glassy with emotion.

"There," Clara said softly, her voice trembling with a mix of satisfaction and apology. "See? Maybe it wasn't what you wanted at first, but… it can still be something beautiful, something memorable."

Nisha staggered back, her hands trembling as she wiped at her lips, her tears flowing freely now. "No," she choked out, her voice raw. "That wasn't beautiful. That wasn't what I wanted! You don't get to decide what's special for me!"

Clara's face fell, guilt finally beginning to register as the spell's haze wavered, but the damage was already done. Nisha's heart raced as she stepped further away, her mind reeling. *I have to get away. I have to figure out how to fix this.*

Nisha swallowed her fear and wiped away her tears, her mind racing for a way out of the situation. Clara, still standing too close, watched her with a mix of longing and confusion, the spell's hold keeping her from leaving on her own.

Taking a deep breath, Nisha forced a small, shaky smile onto her face. "You know what?" she said, her voice trembling but steady enough to sound sincere. "You're right. I should do something to make this moment... better. Let me go get something for you. Flowers! Stay here, and I'll bring you some flowers, okay? Something special."

Clara blinked, her expression softening slightly. The suggestion seemed to soothe her, though the intense glimmer of obsession remained in her eyes. "Flowers?" she repeated, her voice quieter now, almost hesitant. "You'd do that for me?"

"Of course," Nisha said, nodding quickly. "Just wait here, okay? I'll be right back."

Clara hesitated, then slowly nodded, her lips curling into a small smile. "Okay… I'll wait."

Without wasting another second, Nisha turned and walked away, keeping her pace measured until she rounded the corner and was out of Clara's sight. Then, she broke into a run, her heart pounding in her chest as she sprinted away from the bus stop. She didn't stop until she was far from Clara, the tension in her body only slightly easing as the distance grew between them.

Chapter – 3 Sisterly Feelings

By the time Nisha reached her house, she was out of breath and still shaking. She slammed the door behind her and leaned against it, her mind racing with everything that had happened. Her lips still tingled uncomfortably from the forced kiss, and the memory of Clara's obsessive gaze sent shivers down her spine.

Nisha slid down to the floor, burying her face in her hands. "What have I gotten myself into?" she whispered, her voice trembling. The weight of the spell, its consequences, and the terrifying events of the evening felt like too much to handle.

But one thing was clear—she couldn't let this continue. She had to figure out a way to break the spell, no matter what it took.

The sound of Shaya's door creaking open made Nisha's heart stop. She had barely caught her breath from the ordeal with Clara, and now, dread coursed through her veins as her older sister's sharp voice cut through the silence.

"Who's making noise at this hour?" Shaya called, irritation dripping from her tone.

Nisha quickly scrambled to her feet, her mind racing. "It's just me," she replied hastily, trying to sound nonchalant. "Nothing to worry about!"

"Figures," Shaya muttered from behind her closed door, her words laced with disdain. "I'm about to leave. Don't bother me." The sound of footsteps approached the door, and Nisha's stomach twisted in panic.

"Wait, no!" Nisha shouted, her voice trembling as realization struck. "Please, don't come out!" But it was too late.

The door swung open, and Shaya stepped into the hallway, her piercing eyes locking onto Nisha's. Shaya was wearing her usual edgy ensemble: a black leather jacket zipped halfway up over a cropped tank top, paired with tiny denim shorts that showed off her long legs. Her dark hair was tied back in a loose ponytail, and her expression carried its usual air of superiority.

For a moment, Shaya's annoyed scowl remained as she crossed her arms, looking at Nisha as if ready to deliver one of her usual condescending remarks. But then something shifted. Her eyes softened, her mouth parted slightly, and her entire demeanor changed in an instant.

"Wow," Shaya said, her voice dropping to a hushed, almost reverent tone. Her arms fell to her sides, and she took an unconscious step closer to Nisha. Her gaze lingered on Nisha's face, and her lips curled into a faint smile—something Nisha had never seen directed at her before. "You look… amazing."

Nisha's blood ran cold. "Shaya, no," she stammered, backing away. "Don't do this. Don't… feel like this. It's the spell!"

Shaya tilted her head, her expression unusually gentle yet unsettlingly intense. "What are you talking about?" she asked, her voice softer than Nisha had ever heard it. "I've never noticed before, but you're... beautiful, Nisha. Stunning, really."

Her eyes flicked over Nisha's face and down to her trembling hands, her smile deepening. "I don't know why I never realized it before," Shaya murmured, stepping closer, her tone low and inviting, "but there's something about you tonight. Something irresistible."

Nisha backed up until she was pressed against the wall, her heart hammering in her chest.

"This isn't you, Shaya," she said, her voice cracking. "You hate me, remember? You always do! Don't let this... magic mess with your head!"

But Shaya just shook her head slowly, her expression warm and almost tender now. "I don't hate you, Nisha. I could never hate you. In fact..." Her fingers reached out, grazing Nisha's arm lightly, sending a shiver down her spine. "I think I've been wrong about a lot of things."
Nisha's breath hitched as the weight of the situation settled on her shoulders. *This spell is ruining everything,* she thought, panic overtaking her.

Nisha pressed herself against the wall, her hands trembling as she held them up defensively. Her mind raced as she tried to find the words that might break through to Shaya and snap her out of this spell's grip.

"Shaya, think about it!" Nisha exclaimed, her voice high-pitched with desperation. "You hate me! You've always hated me! Just yesterday, you told Mom and Dad I was irresponsible because I was late to class. And before that, you said I was a waste of space, remember? You've always ignored me, bullied me, and treated me like garbage. You don't like me, and you never have!"

For a brief moment, Shaya hesitated, her brow furrowing as if the memories Nisha was bringing up were clashing with her current feelings. But then her expression softened again, her lips curving into a slow, seductive smile. She took another step closer, her hands sliding into the pockets of her leather jacket, her posture relaxed and confident.

"You've got it all wrong, Nisha," Shaya said, her voice dropping into a sultry tone. "Maybe

I've been hard on you, sure. But that's just because I didn't know how to deal with how I really felt. Maybe all this time… I've been pushing you away because I didn't want to admit how much you mean to me."

"What?" Nisha choked, her stomach twisting in disbelief. "No! That's not true! This isn't real, Shaya! It's the spell—nothing about this is real!"

Shaya just chuckled softly, her eyes glinting with a dangerous mix of affection and obsession. "You're wrong," she said, stepping even closer. "This feels more real than anything I've ever known." Her hand reached out, brushing against Nisha's cheek, and Nisha flinched at the touch, her breath catching in her throat.

"Don't fight it," Shaya murmured, leaning in. "You're beautiful, Nisha. I've been such a fool not to see it before." Her other hand trailed down to Nisha's shoulder, and despite Nisha's protests and attempts to push her away, Shaya's grip was firm, her strength undeniable.

Nisha's heart pounded as Shaya closed the gap between them. Her lips brushed against Nisha's, soft but insistent, in a kiss that mirrored Clara's earlier actions. Nisha struggled, her hands pushing weakly against Shaya's chest, but it was no use. The spell's influence had completely overtaken Shaya, just as it had Clara.

"Shaya, please," Nisha mumbled against the kiss, her voice breaking with fear and frustration. But Shaya didn't stop. The kiss deepened, becoming more passionate as Shaya's hands moved to hold Nisha in place.

Nisha's mind raced, tears streaming down her cheeks as she realized she was trapped once again, powerless to stop the magic that had turned her life into a nightmare.

As Shaya's lips pressed against hers, Nisha squirmed, her muffled protests growing more frantic. She tried to turn her face away, her voice trembling and choked with panic. "Shaya, stop!" she mumbled, her words barely audible against the insistent kiss. "I'm your sister! This isn't right! Please, stop!"

The word "sister" seemed to reach Shaya, but instead of snapping her out of the spell, it only made her pause briefly. Her eyes, filled with a dazed intensity, met Nisha's tear-filled gaze. Shaya's expression softened into something that, to Nisha's horror, looked like affectionate indulgence.

"I know," Shaya whispered, her voice low and almost reverent. "But I can't help it, Nisha. I don't want to help it. You're... irresistible. You've always been so beautiful, and now it's like I finally see it. How did I never notice? You... you're incredible, Nisha." Her voice was softer now, almost reverent, as if speaking a truth she'd just discovered I can't stop myself. I don't *want* to stop myself."
Nisha's stomach churned, and fresh tears streamed down her cheeks. She pushed harder against Shaya's chest, her voice rising in desperation. "No! Shaya, listen to yourself! This isn't you! This is some... awful magic! You don't feel this way, not really! You're my *sister*! This is wrong, please!"

Shaya didn't respond with words. Instead, she leaned back in, her touch more tender yet just as overwhelming, as if she believed her actions could convey something Nisha's words couldn't change. Nisha twisted her head away, her tears wetting her cheeks as she struggled against the overwhelming weight of the spell's consequences.

Inside, Nisha's heart shattered as she realized how deep the magic's hold was—so strong it twisted even the most sacred of bonds into something unrecognizable.

Nisha's voice rose in a mix of shock and disbelief as she tried to push Shaya away again, her words tumbling out in a frantic rush. "Oh my God! Until yesterday, I'd never been kissed—*not once*! And now, today, I've been kissed by *two women*! And one of them is my *sister*! What the hell is happening?"

Shaya paused for a brief moment, her lips curling into a smirk. The glint in her eyes was both amused and maddeningly unshaken. "Well," she said with a low chuckle, her voice laced with an unsettling mixture of humor and seduction, "I guess you're just a late bloomer, Nisha. Better late than never, right?"

Nisha's stomach twisted at the flippancy of the response, and before she could say anything, Shaya's hands moved to the hem of Nisha's white top. With unnerving confidence, Shaya began to lift the fabric, her touch firm yet surprisingly gentle and suddenly she had removed Nisha's top and threw it away.

"Stop it!" Nisha screamed, grabbing at Shaya's wrists and trying to pull them away. Her voice was high-pitched and desperate, her body trembling as she fought against her sister's actions. "Shaya, what are you doing? This is insane! You're my sister!"

But Shaya's smirk only deepened, as if she found Nisha's protests charming rather than alarming. "Relax," she said smoothly, her tone almost teasing. "You'll feel better if you stop fighting it. I know I do."

Nisha's heart pounded as she struggled harder, her tears streaming freely now. "No! You're not thinking straight! This isn't real—it's the spell! Please, Shaya, stop!"

But the spell's influence had warped Shaya's thoughts completely, twisting her perception into something unrecognizable. Nisha's pleas seemed to bounce off her, unheard and unheeded.

Nisha's heart pounded as adrenaline surged through her veins. Summoning all her strength, she twisted out of Shaya's grip and darted toward the door. Shaya called out, her voice still laced with that unnerving, spell-driven affection, but Nisha didn't stop. She threw herself out of the house, slamming the door shut behind her.

With shaking hands, she locked the door, turning the latch and pressing her back against the wooden frame. Her chest heaved as she tried to catch her breath, the cool night air biting against her skin.

It wasn't until the chill sank in that Nisha glanced down and realized, with horror, that she was standing outside in nothing but her black bra. Her white top, the one Shaya had seductively removed, was still inside the house—inside with Shaya.

Her cheeks flushed with embarrassment and panic as she wrapped her arms around herself, shivering in the cool evening breeze. The street was quiet, but she knew it was only a matter of time before someone passed by, and the thought of being seen like this sent her anxiety skyrocketing.

From inside, Shaya's muffled voice called through the door. "Nisha, come on," she said, her tone sweet yet disturbingly possessive. "Don't leave me like this. Let me help you. You know I only want what's best for you…"

Nisha pressed her hands over her ears, her tears threatening to spill again. This is a nightmare, she thought. I need to fix this, but how?

Chapter – 4 Elma, the Garbage Lady

Nisha looked around desperately, her arms still crossed over her chest to cover herself. That's when she spotted Elma, the elderly sweeper who worked in the neighborhood and had been a familiar presence in Nisha's life since she was a child. Elma, now in her early sixties, was trudging down the street with a garbage bag slung over her shoulder, her weathered face illuminated by the faint glow of a nearby streetlamp. She wore a plain, faded floral dress and a cardigan that looked like it had seen better days, along with sturdy boots that clunked softly against the pavement.

Elma was kind and had always greeted Nisha with a warm smile whenever they crossed paths. At that moment, she felt like the only person who could help.

"Elma!" Nisha called out, her voice shaking with a mix of relief and embarrassment as she jogged toward her.

The old woman turned, squinting through her wire-rimmed glasses. When she saw Nisha, her face registered shock. "Nisha, child, what on earth are you doing out here like that?" she exclaimed, her voice heavy with concern as she hurried over, dropping her garbage bag.

"I—I need your help," Nisha stammered, trying to keep her voice steady despite the tears pricking at her eyes. "Something happened, and I don't have my top. Please, Elma, can you lend me something to wear? Anything?"

Elma frowned, glancing around the quiet street as if checking to make sure no one else was watching. "Good heavens, child," she muttered, shrugging off her cardigan and holding it out to Nisha. "Here, take this. Cover yourself up before you catch a cold—or worse, someone else sees you like this."

Nisha quickly wrapped the cardigan around herself, the scratchy fabric a welcome shield against the night air. "Thank you," she said, her voice barely above a whisper. "Thank you so much."

Elma studied her with a mix of concern and curiosity. "Now, what's going on, Nisha?" she asked, her voice gentle but firm. "Why are you out here like this? And why do you look like you've been crying?"

Nisha hesitated, her mind racing. She trusted Elma, but how could she explain something as bizarre and unbelievable as a spell turning everyone who saw her into an obsessed admirer?

Nisha took a deep breath, preparing to explain, but before she could speak, she noticed a subtle shift in Elma's demeanor. The concern in the old woman's eyes softened, replaced by a strange, lingering gaze that sent a chill down Nisha's spine.

"Elma?" Nisha asked cautiously, pulling the cardigan tighter around herself. "Are you okay?"

Elma blinked a few times, as if shaking off a haze, but when her eyes met Nisha's again, they held an intensity that wasn't there before. She reached out, her hand brushing against Nisha's arm in a way that felt oddly tender. "I'm fine, sweetheart," she said softly, her voice unusually warm. "It's just... you've grown up so beautifully, Nisha. I don't think I've ever noticed before."

Nisha's heart sank as realization struck. *No... not Elma too.*

"Thanks," Nisha said quickly, taking a step back, but Elma followed, her movements slow and deliberate, her eyes never leaving Nisha's face.

"You're such a sweet girl," Elma continued, her tone growing softer, almost wistful. "Always have been. But now, there's something about you... something so radiant, so... captivating." She hesitated, her hand lingering near Nisha's arm. "I don't know why, but I feel drawn to you in a way I can't explain."

"Elma, stop," Nisha said, her voice trembling. "This isn't you. It's… it's something else, something wrong. Please, just… step back."

But Elma didn't listen. Instead, she smiled faintly, her cheeks flushing as she stepped closer. Her fingers brushed against Nisha's hand, and her touch felt heavier, more deliberate. "Don't be afraid, darling," she said gently. "I just want to help you… take care of you. I've always cared about you, Nisha. You know that."

Nisha's stomach twisted in panic as Elma's behavior grew increasingly unsettling. The kind, maternal figure she had known her entire life was now looking at her with an affection that was far too intense, far too… intimate.

"Elma, no," Nisha said, backing away again. "You're not thinking clearly. This isn't real! Please, just leave me alone!"
But the spell's hold on Elma had already taken root. Her voice dropped to a whisper, her tone almost reverent. "You're so beautiful, Nisha. Like an angel. I can't believe I never saw it before…"

Elma stepped closer, her movements slow and deliberate, and Nisha felt the panic rising in her chest once again. She had to do something before the situation spiraled even further out of control.

Elma's expression softened into something disturbingly tender as she reached out and gently tugged at the cardigan she had just given Nisha. "You don't need this," she murmured, her voice low and soothing, though her actions were anything but. "Let me see you properly. You're too beautiful to hide."

"No! Elma, stop!" Nisha protested, clutching the cardigan tightly against herself, but Elma's hands were insistent. With surprising strength, the older woman pulled the cardigan off Nisha's shoulders, leaving her exposed once again in her lingerie.

"You're breathtaking, sweetheart," Elma said, her voice thick with emotion as she looked at Nisha like she was the most precious thing she had ever seen. Her weathered hands cupped Nisha's face, her touch tender yet firm, her thumbs brushing away Nisha's tears. "Don't cry, my darling. You don't need to be afraid. I'll take care of you."

Nisha struggled, her body trembling as Elma leaned in closer, her breath warm against Nisha's skin. "Elma, please," she pleaded, her voice breaking. "You've known me since I was a kid! This isn't right—it's the spell! You're not yourself!"

But Elma didn't seem to hear her. Her gaze was filled with a longing that Nisha had never seen before, and it terrified her. "Hush," Elma whispered, her voice both soothing and commanding. "You're so special, Nisha. So precious. Let me show you how much I care for you."

Nisha gasped as Elma's lips met hers, the kiss far more deliberate and practiced than the others had been. Elma's touch was experienced and confident, her hands moving to hold Nisha steady as the kiss deepened. Nisha tried to twist away, but Elma's grip was firm, her actions driven by the spell's overpowering influence.

The intensity of the moment was suffocating, and Nisha's protests were muffled against Elma's lips. The older woman's experience made her actions more calculated, more knowing, and it left Nisha feeling utterly trapped. Tears streamed down her cheeks as she squirmed in Elma's hold, but the spell's pull on the woman was too strong, and her affection too overwhelming.

Nisha's heart raced as she realized the situation was spiraling further out of control, and she had to find a way to break free before things went any further.

Nisha sprinted through the quiet streets, her heart pounding and her mind racing as she fought back tears of fear and frustration. Her bare arms were chilled in the cool night air, and every shadow seemed to loom larger, as if the world itself was conspiring against her. Finally, she spotted the familiar steeple of the church near her home—a place she had always considered safe.

Chapter – 5 The Holy Church

She pushed open the heavy wooden doors and stumbled inside, her breath coming in ragged gasps. The church was dimly lit, candles flickering along the altar and casting dancing shadows across the walls. The air smelled faintly of incense, a soothing balm to her frayed nerves.

An aged man, the church's padri, appeared from one of the side rooms. He was a kindly figure, with a weathered face and a gentle smile. His clerical robes swayed softly as he approached her, his voice calm and reassuring. "Child," he said, his tone filled with concern, "what brings you here at this hour? You look distressed. Come, sit down."

Nisha hesitated but then allowed herself to be guided to a wooden pew. The padri draped a shawl over her shoulders before disappearing into a small room. He returned moments later with a simple white top, which he handed to her. "Here, put this on. It's not much, but it will keep you covered."

"Thank you," Nisha said softly, quickly pulling the top over her head. The fabric was rough but comforting, and she felt slightly less exposed.

The padri sat beside her, his kind eyes searching her face. "You are safe here, child," he said gently. "Whatever has happened to you, we can help. I'll fetch Nun Aasha. She is wise and compassionate. She will know what to do."

At the mention of a nun, Nisha's heart raced. She shook her head quickly, her voice trembling. "No, I don't need a nun. Please, don't call her."

The padri frowned slightly, his confusion evident. "But why, my dear? Aasha is a woman of God, dedicated to her faith. She has no worldly desires—she is beyond such things. If you are afraid, rest assured that no harm will come to you under her care."

Nisha hesitated. She wanted to believe him, wanted to trust that the spell's reach couldn't penetrate the sanctity of the church or affect someone so devoted. Slowly, she nodded. "Okay," she said softly. "If you're sure."

The padri smiled warmly. "You'll see. She will bring you peace."

He stood and disappeared down a side hallway, leaving Nisha alone for a moment in the quiet church. She closed her eyes and tried to steady her breathing, hoping against hope that this would finally be the refuge she so desperately needed.

Moments later, soft footsteps echoed through the hall as the padri returned, accompanied by Nun Aasha. She was a serene woman in her late forties, her face framed by the white and black of her habit. Her expression was calm, her eyes kind as she approached.
"Child," Aasha said gently, her voice like a soothing melody. "What troubles you? How can I help?"

Nisha opened her mouth to respond, but as Nun Aasha stepped closer, the faint glow of the candles seemed to catch her eyes differently. Her calm expression faltered, her gaze lingering on Nisha for a moment too long.

Nisha's stomach twisted. *No. No, no, no...* she thought, realizing with dread that the spell was beginning to work.

Nun Aasha's serene demeanor shifted slightly, her kind smile taking on a strange, almost reverent quality. "You..." she said softly, her voice trailing off. Her hands trembled faintly as she clasped them in front of her, her gaze fixed on Nisha with an intensity that hadn't been there moments before.

Nisha's heart sank as the spell's inevitable power began to take hold, leaving her once again trapped in its unrelenting grasp.

The padri furrowed his brow as he noticed Nun Aasha's unusual demeanor. Her normally serene expression was now tinged with something he couldn't quite place—something almost... enthralled. He stepped closer, his voice calm but firm.

"Aasha," he said, his tone laced with concern, "what are you doing? Why are you looking at the girl like that?"

Nun Aasha hesitated, blinking as though she was trying to gather her thoughts. Her hands unclasped, one drifting to her chest as if to steady herself. She took a deep breath, but when she looked back at Nisha, the intensity in her gaze only deepened.

"I don't know," Aasha admitted softly, her voice trembling slightly. "There's something about her. She's… radiant. Beautiful beyond words. It's like she carries a divine light within her."

The padri frowned, his confusion growing. "Aasha, what are you saying? You're speaking nonsense." He looked back at Nisha, then at Aasha again, his concern deepening.

But Aasha shook her head, her movements slow and deliberate. She stepped closer to Nisha, her eyes filled with a mix of awe and longing. "No, it's not nonsense," she insisted, her voice now reverent. "There's something extraordinary about her. I feel it in my soul. I can't look away… I can't stop…" Her words trailed off, her cheeks flushing faintly.

Nisha stood frozen, her stomach twisting in dread as Aasha's words confirmed her worst fears.

"It's the spell," Nisha blurted out, her voice shaky. "This isn't you, Aasha. It's magic—it's making you feel this way. Please, fight it!"

The padri turned to Nisha, his expression filled with confusion and disbelief. "Magic? What are you talking about, child?"

But Nun Aasha wasn't listening anymore. She took another step toward Nisha, her breath shallow, her trembling hand reaching out as though compelled by an unseen force. Her voice dropped to a whisper, heavy with emotion. "I've never felt like this before. It's… overwhelming. I want to protect you, to care for you, to… be near you."

"Aasha!" the padri said sharply, stepping between her and Nisha. His stern tone seemed to snap her out of her trance briefly, and she blinked, confusion flickering across her face.
But as her gaze returned to Nisha, the spell's hold grew stronger, and the look in her eyes became even more intense. "I can't help it," Aasha said, her voice breaking. "I've never felt anything so powerful in my life. It's like she's a miracle walking among us…"

Nisha's heart raced as the situation spiraled further out of control. *Not here too. Not in the church,* she thought, her panic growing with every passing second.

Nun Aasha's breathing quickened as the spell's overwhelming compulsion took full control. Her trembling hands clenched at her sides for a brief moment, but the tension gave way as she stepped forward with newfound determination. Her gaze was locked on Nisha, her expression a mixture of reverence, desire, and something almost predatory.

"Aasha, stop this madness!" the padri exclaimed, his voice shaking with disbelief as he moved to intercept her. But Aasha, consumed by the spell, shoved him aside with surprising strength.

He stumbled backward, falling into a nearby chair. His head struck the wooden frame, and he slumped forward, dazed and groaning faintly, his attempts to intervene silenced.

Nisha's heart pounded in terror as Aasha turned back to her, her hands trembling yet steady as they reached out. "You don't understand, child," Aasha murmured, her voice thick with emotion. "You're more than human… you're divine. A miracle. I've never felt anything like this. You're so beautiful, so perfect… I have to be near you."

"Aasha, please," Nisha whimpered, backing away until she felt the cold stone wall of the church behind her. "This isn't real! It's not you! It's some kind of spell—it's making you feel this way!"

But Aasha didn't seem to hear her. She was completely consumed, her eyes glassy with obsession. Her hands gently but firmly took hold of Nisha's arms, pulling her forward. Her touch was reverent, almost worshipful, but her grip was unyielding.

"Nisha," Aasha whispered, her face close enough that Nisha could feel her breath. "You don't understand the gift you've been given. You're… irresistible. You're everything." Her trembling fingers brushed Nisha's cheek, sending an involuntary shiver through her.

"Let me show you," Aasha murmured, her voice soft and tender yet tinged with an unsettling intensity. She leaned in, her lips brushing against Nisha's in a kiss that was both gentle and possessive. Nisha froze, her body stiff as she felt Aasha's experienced, deliberate movements.

Unlike the others, Aasha's actions were not hesitant or uncertain—they were confident, her lips moving with an almost practiced devotion.

Nisha squirmed, her hands weakly pushing against Aasha's shoulders, but the nun was unfazed, her hands moving to cradle Nisha's face. The kiss deepened, becoming more fervent, her touch traveling down Nisha's arms and sending waves of discomfort and helplessness through her.

"Aasha, stop," Nisha mumbled against the kiss, her voice muffled and broken by her own sobs. But Aasha didn't stop. Her hands slid down to Nisha's waist, holding her firmly as though afraid she might slip away.

The sacred air of the church was heavy with an unbearable tension as Nisha's muffled cries echoed faintly. The flickering candlelight cast distorted shadows on the walls, as if the very space itself bore witness to the horrifying twist of fate.

Nisha's tears streamed freely now, her body trembling as she tried to twist away. The sense of safety she had sought in the church was now completely shattered, and the realization that even this holy place could not protect her left her feeling utterly hopeless. *There's no escaping this spell,* she thought, panic rising in her chest. *It's turning everyone into someone I don't recognize...*

Aasha tries to expose Nisha by shredding off any cloth she has on. Nisha resists at first but as Aasha was strong and so that she does not get hurt she gives into Aasha's temptation.

Nisha's pulse raced as Aasha's actions became more intense, and the desperation to escape surged through her. She pushed against Aasha's hands, using all the strength she could muster. "No! Stop it!" Nisha cried, her voice breaking with fear and anger. "Let me go!"

But Aasha, under the influence of the spell, held on firmly, her obsession overpowering any sense of rationality. Nisha knew she had to think quickly. She twisted her body sharply, slipping out of Aasha's grasp just enough to duck beneath her arms. With a burst of adrenaline, she bolted toward the nearest aisle of the church, her bare feet echoing loudly against the stone floor.

"Come back, Nisha!" Aasha called, her voice a mixture of longing and urgency as she stumbled after her. "Please, I only want to care for you!"

Nisha didn't look back. Her heart pounded in her chest as she scanned the dimly lit church for an exit. The heavy wooden doors were too far, and she knew Aasha would catch up to her if she went straight for them. Instead, she spotted a side door near the altar—a narrow, unassuming passage that might lead to safety.

She sprinted toward it and took her clothes lying down which Aasha removed. Her breaths coming in ragged gasps as she fumbled with the latch. Her hands trembled, but with a desperate yank, she managed to pull the door open. The cool night air rushed in, and she didn't hesitate for a second. She darted through the doorway and into the dark alley behind the church.

The sounds of Aasha's footsteps faded as the door swung shut behind her. Nisha didn't stop running, her bare feet pounding against the rough pavement as she pushed herself forward, her lungs burning with exertion. She didn't know where she was going, but she knew she had to put as much distance as possible between herself and anyone who might succumb to the spell.

Tears blurred her vision as she whispered to herself, "I have to find a way to end this. I have to fix this before it destroys me completely."

The darkened streets stretched out before her, offering no sign of solace or safety, but Nisha forced herself to keep moving, her mind racing with thoughts of what to do next.

Chapter – 6 Self Reflection

As Nisha slowed her pace, her breaths coming in ragged gasps, she leaned against the rough brick wall of an alley, her body trembling. The cool night air chilled her skin, and the overwhelming events of the day came crashing down on her. Her mind was a chaotic mess of fear, confusion, and a profound sense of violation.

Before today, she had never been kissed.

The thought struck her like a heavy weight, and she sank to the ground, pulling her knees up to her chest. Her fingers brushed against her lips, which still felt raw and unfamiliar from the day's encounters. Her tears welled up as she whispered to herself, "I've never felt a kiss before today… and now…"

She trailed off, her mind recounting the surreal, nightmarish moments that had unfolded.

1. **Clara**, the stranger at the bus stop, had been the first. Her kiss had been intense and unwanted, fueled by the overwhelming pull of the spell.
2. Then there was **Shaya**, her own sister, whose kiss had left Nisha feeling more trapped and betrayed than she thought possible.
3. Then **Elma**, the woman she knew from her childhood who forgot all her maternal instincts and just pounded over Nisha like a lust lady.
4. And finally, **Aasha**, the serene and devout nun, whose actions in the church had shattered any hope that sanctity could protect her from the spell's reach.

Four women. Four experiences that left her vulnerable and shaken, their intensity escalating each time.

"Why is this happening to me?" Nisha muttered, her voice trembling. "I didn't want this. I didn't ask for any of this." She wiped her tears roughly with the back of her hand, but they kept falling, her emotions spiraling out of control.

She thought about the life she had before today, a life that now felt so distant. A quiet existence where she had daydreamed about her first kiss being with the boy she had a crush on, where intimacy felt like something to look forward to—not something to fear. That world was gone now, replaced by a terrifying new reality where her every interaction with another woman felt like a ticking time bomb.

"I've been kissed more times today than I ever imagined," she whispered bitterly. "And none of it felt like it was mine."
The thought made her feel hollow, as though something had been stolen from her, leaving behind a painful void. She hugged her knees tighter, trying to steady her breathing. "I need to fix this," she said quietly to herself, her voice trembling but determined. "I can't let this go on. There has to be a way to undo this spell."

Nisha's trembling fingers gripped her knees tightly as fragments of the day began to resurface, blurry memories sharpening into terrifying clarity. Vashika's words echoed in her mind, cutting through her thoughts like a blade.

"At first, you will resist the kiss... but later, you will long for it. You will want more."

Her breath hitched as the realization dawned on her. This spell wasn't just manipulating those around her—it was working its way into her own thoughts, her own actions, without her even realizing it. She pressed her hands to her temples, her body shaking as the memories became painfully vivid.

Clara. The memory of the first kiss came flooding back. Nisha had been stunned and horrified at the time, but now she recalled something she hadn't fully registered then. After Clara kissed her, she had felt an odd, inexplicable pull. Her initial resistance had faded, and a strange, overwhelming desire had taken its place. She had lunged toward Clara, her hands clutching at her, her voice trembling with unbidden words.

"I want you more," she had whispered, her voice husky and desperate, her body pressing against Clara's as though she couldn't bear to let her go. Her lips had sought Clara's again, her own actions alien to her, as if her body was no longer her own.

Shaya. The scene with her sister burned in her mind now, the details painfully clear. She had resisted at first, begging Shaya to stop, but then, when she was pushed against the wall, something inside her had shifted. Her own hands had moved to her top, pulling it off and exposing herself willingly.

"I want you more than anyone," she had murmured, her voice thick with longing. Her hands had reached for Shaya, pulling her closer, her body moving of its own accord. The desperation in her voice, the heat of her touch—it wasn't her, but it had felt so real in the moment.

Elma. The sweeper. Nisha's chest tightened as she remembered giving back the cardigan she had clung to for warmth. She had handed it over without hesitation, her hands trembling not with fear, but with something darker. She could now recall the way she had leaned into the older woman's kiss, her lips moving in sync, her breath hitching not in panic, but in anticipation.

"I want you more than you want me," she had whispered, her voice dripping with need. Her hands had clung to Elma's shoulders, her body pressing against the sweeper as though craving her touch.

Aasha. Nisha's breath hitched as the memory of the church returned, the sacred setting twisting in her mind like a cruel joke. She had removed the white top that the padri had given her, pulling it over her head and letting it drop to the floor without hesitation. Her voice had been soft, pleading, filled with desire as she leaned toward the nun.

"I want you more," she had said, her words cutting through the heavy air of the church. "Please, Aasha... don't stop." Her hands had moved to Aasha's waist, pulling her closer, her actions driven by a force she hadn't even been aware of at the time.

Nisha's eyes widened as these horrifying realizations sank in. Her hands trembled violently, her chest rising and falling with shallow breaths. "No," she whispered, her voice breaking. "No, no, no... that wasn't me. I didn't... I wouldn't..."

But the memories felt too vivid, too real. She had resisted at first, yes—but then she had given in. Not just given in, but *participated*. Her own voice, her own hands, her own body had betrayed her, succumbing to the spell's insidious influence.

"What's happening to me?" she whispered, her tears falling freely now. "How could I... how did I...?"

Her mind raced, panic clawing at her as she realized the spell wasn't just controlling others—it was controlling *her*. Twisting her thoughts, her desires, her very actions into something unrecognizable.

I need to stop this, she thought, her heart pounding. *I need to find a way to end this before it destroys me completely.*

Nisha sat trembling in the dark alley, her mind racing as she pieced together the horrifying truth. The spell wasn't just corrupting those around her—it was invading her, burrowing into her thoughts and actions. It was twisting her emotions, her will, until she couldn't tell where her own choices ended and the spell's influence began. She gripped her head in her hands, tears streaming down her face.

I have to end this, she thought, her resolve hardening despite the fear clutching at her heart. *Before it consumes me entirely.*

She stood up shakily, her bare feet aching from the rough pavement, and wiped her face with trembling hands. There was only one person who might have the answers she needed: Vashika. The crystal ball reader who had cast the spell. Nisha's fists clenched as anger replaced her tears. Vashika had manipulated her, deceived her—and now, she was the only one who could undo this nightmare.

"I'm going back to her," Nisha muttered to herself, her voice trembling but resolute. "She started this, and she's going to fix it."

Nisha retraced her steps through the quiet, empty streets, her body tense with every shadow that flickered in the dim light. The events of the night replayed in her mind like a haunting melody: Clara, Shaya, Elma, Aasha. Each memory felt like a scar, a reminder of how much control she had lost. But she pushed forward, her determination growing with every step.

Finally, the familiar, eerie silhouette of Vashika's cottage came into view. The windows glowed faintly, the light inside flickering like a living thing. Nisha hesitated for only a moment before marching up the dirt path and pounding on the door with both fists.

Chapter – 7 Confrontation with Vashika

"Vashika!" she shouted, her voice echoing in the stillness. "Open up! I know you're in there!"

The door creaked open slowly, and Vashika appeared, her dark eyes glittering with that same mysterious glint. She looked calm, almost pleased, as if she had been expecting Nisha's return.

"Ah, my dear," Vashika said softly, her lips curling into a faint smile. "You're back. I had a feeling you might return."

Nisha stormed inside, her fear giving way to raw anger. "What did you do to me?" she demanded, her voice trembling. "You didn't tell me the truth about the spell! It's not just making them obsessed—it's changing *me*! It's making me do things I would never do!"

Vashika closed the door behind them with a slow, deliberate motion and turned to face

Nisha. Her smile didn't waver, but her eyes glimmered with something deeper—something almost predatory. "Ah," she said, her voice smooth and unbothered. "So you've noticed."

"Noticed?" Nisha spat, her fists clenching. "You mean how I've been… acting? How I've been saying things, doing things that aren't *me*? You knew this would happen, didn't you? You planned it!"

Vashika stepped closer, her movements graceful, almost hypnotic. "Of course, I knew," she said calmly. "The spell isn't just about them, dear Nisha. It's about you. Desire flows both ways—it's a dance, not a one-sided performance. You wanted to draw others to you, but for that to happen, you had to… open yourself to them. Fully."

Nisha's stomach twisted, and she stepped back, her breathing ragged. "No! I didn't agree to this! I didn't agree to lose myself!"

Vashika chuckled softly, her voice low and melodic. "You wanted power, Nisha. Power comes with a price. And whether you realize it or not, you've been enjoying it. Have you not?"

Nisha shook her head violently, her voice breaking. "No! I hate it! I hate all of it! Undo it! End the spell!"

Vashika tilted her head, her smile fading into something more serious. "End it?" she repeated, her tone thoughtful. "Oh, Nisha, it's not so simple. Magic like this doesn't just vanish. It must be… transferred."

Nisha froze. "Transferred? What does that mean?"
Vashika' gaze darkened, and she leaned in closer, her voice dropping to a whisper. "If you truly wish to be free of the spell, you must pass it on to someone else. Let them carry its weight. Only then will you be free."

Nisha's heart sank as the full weight of Vashika ' words hit her. *Pass it on? To someone else?* She clenched her fists, her mind racing with the implications.
"Who?" she asked, her voice shaking. "Who would I even…?"

Vashika smiled faintly, stepping back. "That, my dear, is entirely up to you."

Nisha's world spun as she grappled with the impossible choice before her. The nightmare wasn't over—if anything, it had just begun.

Nisha's voice trembled as she spoke, her hands balled into fists at her sides. "Even if I decide who to transfer this to—which is horrible enough—how would I even *do* it? How do you transfer a spell like this?"

Vashika smiled faintly, her dark eyes glittering with mystery. She walked slowly to the crystal ball on the center table, her hands hovering above it as it began to glow faintly, swirling with hues of deep purple and blue. "The transfer is simple in its mechanics," she said softly, her voice like a low hum. "You must willingly pass the spell to another. A kiss seals the transfer—a conscious choice on your part."

Nisha's stomach dropped. "A… kiss?" she repeated, her voice barely above a whisper.

Vashika nodded, her gaze unwavering. "Yes. The same kiss that once ensnared you can set you free. But it must be done with intent. The transfer is only successful if your heart and mind align—if you truly wish to rid yourself of the spell and give it to another."

Nisha stared at her, her chest tightening as the weight of the revelation pressed down on her. "So, I'd have to… curse someone else? Make them go through what I've been through?"

"Precisely," Vashika said smoothly. "The burden must be carried by someone. Magic like this does not simply dissipate—it needs a host. That is the nature of such power. But once it leaves you, it will be theirs to bear."

Nisha felt like the floor was crumbling beneath her. "That's… that's monstrous!" she exclaimed, tears springing to her eyes. "How could I do that to someone? How could I *choose* to ruin someone else's life like mine has been ruined?"

Vashika tilted her head, her smile faint but unrelenting. "And yet, here you stand, desperate for freedom. Ask yourself, Nisha—how long can you live like this? How many more lives will the spell ruin while it remains bound to you? Perhaps it's better to place it in the hands of someone stronger, someone who might wield it with purpose… or simply live with the consequences better than you."

Nisha's breath hitched as she backed away from the crystal ball, her thoughts spinning in a chaotic storm. The idea of passing the spell to another felt unthinkable, but so did living with it forever.

Vashika' voice softened, almost coaxing. "You have a choice, dear Nisha. Embrace the power… or pass it on. Either way, the decision is yours to make."
Nisha stood frozen, tears streaming down her cheeks as the impossible choice loomed before her.

Vashika watched Nisha with a knowing smirk, her hands resting lightly on the glowing crystal ball. The silence between them was thick and heavy, broken only by Nisha's shallow breaths as she grappled with the enormity of the decision before her.

After a moment, Vashika tilted her head, her voice soft but laced with a sharp edge. "Or perhaps," she said slowly, her words curling through the air like smoke, "you don't truly want to transfer the spell. Perhaps you're not as desperate as you claim to be."

Nisha's head snapped up, her tear-streaked face twisting in confusion and anger. "What are you talking about?" she demanded, her voice breaking.

Vashika's dark eyes glinted with something unreadable, her smile widening ever so slightly. "Oh, come now," she said, her tone mocking yet calm. "You say you hate it, that you're a victim—but are you? Really?"

Nisha shook her head violently, her voice rising. "Of course, I hate it! I didn't ask for this—I never wanted any of this!"

"Didn't you?" Vashika replied, her voice cutting through Nisha's protests like a knife. "Let's reflect for a moment, shall we? You came to me wanting power. You wanted to be noticed, adored, craved. And now… you have it. Perhaps more than you bargained for, yes, but isn't it interesting how quickly you've adapted?"

"I haven't—!" Nisha began, but Vashika raised a hand, silencing her.

"You resisted at first, yes," Vashika continued smoothly. "But then? The spell didn't just affect them, did it? It affected you. And yet, you played along. You said the words. You acted the part. Tell me, Nisha—how much of it was the spell, and how much of it was you?"

"That's not fair!" Nisha shouted, her voice cracking. "I didn't want to—"

"Didn't you?" Vashika interrupted, stepping closer. Her voice softened, but her words carried a weight that bore down on Nisha's chest. "Or do you enjoy it, just a little? The attention. The devotion. The power. Maybe you like playing the victim because it makes you feel… special."

Nisha froze, her mind reeling as those words hit her like a thunderclap. The moments she had tried to forget rushed back to her—the way her body had moved, the words she had spoken, the feelings she couldn't explain. The spell had manipulated her, yes, but there had been flashes, brief moments when she had felt… something. A flicker of satisfaction. A surge of power.

"No," Nisha whispered, shaking her head. "That's not true. I didn't… I wouldn't…"

Vashika leaned in, her voice a low murmur. "Are you sure, dear Nisha? Or perhaps you've already made your choice. You're just too afraid to admit it."

Nisha's knees felt weak as she stumbled back, her chest heaving with panicked breaths. *Am I enjoying this?* she thought, the question twisting her stomach in knots. *No. No, I can't be. I hate this… don't I?*

She stared at Vashika, the room spinning around her as doubt crept into her heart.

Nisha's voice quivered as she stepped forward, her eyes wide and desperate, filled with a mix of fear and confusion. "Isn't there *any* other way to end this?" she pleaded, her hands trembling at her sides. "I don't want to give this curse to someone else. There has to be another way… please."

Vashika's smile faded, replaced by a thoughtful expression as she studied Nisha carefully. She circled her slowly, her dark eyes flickering with a mixture of amusement and something far more dangerous. "There is… another way," she said softly, her voice laced with intrigue. "But it's not for the faint of heart."

Nisha's breath hitched. "What is it?" she asked quickly, her voice trembling with a mix of hope and dread.

Vashika stopped in front of her, leaning in close enough that Nisha could feel the heat of her presence. Her smile returned, sly and seductive. "To rid yourself of the spell without passing it to another, you must burn it out of your soul. This requires you to confront it fully, to embrace the power of the spell until it has no choice but to dissolve within you. To overpower it with your will."

Nisha blinked, her mind racing. "Confront it? How? What does that even mean?"

Vashika's gaze deepened, her tone growing softer, more enticing. "The spell thrives on desire, Nisha. On the passions it stirs in others… and in you. If you wish to break it, you must step into its embrace willingly. Let it consume you completely—body, mind, and soul—until there is no part of you it can control anymore."

Nisha's heart pounded. "Consume me? How? What are you talking about?"

Vashika stepped closer, her fingers brushing against Nisha's cheek, sending a shiver through her. "You must indulge it, darling," she murmured, her voice dripping with temptation. "Give in to every craving, every urge it awakens in you. Love, lust, longing… let them all course through you, freely and completely, without resistance. Embrace the spell so fully that it burns itself out. Only then will you be free."

Nisha's cheeks flushed, her mind reeling at the implications of Vashika ' words. "That sounds… impossible," she stammered. "And dangerous."

"Of course, it's dangerous," Vashika said with a smirk. "But you didn't come to me for safety, did you? You wanted something extraordinary… and this, my dear, is as extraordinary as it gets." Her eyes glittered as she leaned closer, her voice dropping to a low purr. "But if you succeed, you'll emerge more powerful than you've ever imagined. Not cursed. Liberated."

Nisha's knees felt weak as she tried to process what Vashika was saying. The idea of giving in to the spell, of letting it take over completely, terrified her. But a small, rebellious part of her was drawn to the possibility—the chance to finally take control, to be free on her own terms.

"What happens if I fail?" Nisha whispered, her voice barely audible.

Vashika's smile grew wider, more wicked. "Oh, darling," she said softly. "If you fail, you'll lose yourself to the spell entirely. Forever."

The words hung in the air like a storm cloud, their weight pressing down on Nisha as she tried to make sense of the impossible choice before her.

Nisha's body tensed as Vashika's words settled over her like a heavy fog. The spell's grip on her life was unbearable, and yet, the solution Vashika proposed felt equally daunting—if not more so. She swallowed hard, her voice trembling as she asked, "What do you mean? How do I… give into the spell entirely? How do I let it consume me?"

Vashika's smile widened, sly and filled with a mischievous glint that made Nisha's stomach twist. "Ah, my darling," she purred, her voice honeyed and smooth, "it's not something you can do alone. No… you need guidance. You need someone to lead you through the fire, to ensure that you don't falter. And who better to help than the one who cast the spell?"

Nisha's eyes widened in confusion and apprehension. "You? What are you saying? How would you…?"

Vashika chuckled softly, her dark eyes glimmering with an enigmatic intensity. "You must embrace the very thing you fear. Let go of your resistance. Indulge in the desires the spell awakens. But you'll need a partner to help you navigate this… journey. Someone who understands the spell's power." She stepped closer, her movements graceful and deliberate, until the space between them was almost nonexistent. "Come closer to me, Nisha," she murmured, her tone low and inviting. "I will help you."

Nisha's breath hitched, her heart pounding in her chest. Every instinct told her to step back, to run, but something about Vashika ' presence, her commanding gaze, made her feel frozen in place. "Why you?" she whispered, her voice barely audible. "Why would you want to… help me?"

Vashika tilted her head, her smile softening but remaining just as calculated. "Because, my dear, I see your potential. You came to me seeking something extraordinary, and now it's time for you to step into that power. I know the spell—I crafted it. And I can help you master it, but only if you trust me."

Nisha's mind raced, torn between the desire to believe Vashika and the nagging suspicion that this was another manipulation, another trap. Yet, the intensity of Vashika's gaze pulled at her, making it hard to think clearly. She felt the faint warmth of the spell stirring inside her, coaxing her toward the promise of release and freedom.

"Come," Vashika said again, her voice like a soft melody. She extended a hand, her smile widening ever so slightly. "Take the first step, Nisha. Let me show you how to truly embrace the power within you."

The room seemed to grow warmer, the air thicker, as if the very space around them was charged with the spell's energy. Nisha stood frozen, caught between fear, distrust, and the faint, dangerous allure of the promise Vashika offered.

Vashika asked Nisha to recollect the kisses you had with Clara, Shaya, Elma and Aasha. Tell me how all the kisses were. Tell me the qualities you liked about each person with each kiss and then tell me which one was the best?

Nisha's breath hitched as Vashika's words sent a wave of discomfort washing over her. Recollecting the kisses wasn't something she wanted to do—it felt intrusive, overwhelming—but the weight of Vashika's gaze made it hard to resist. The spell still lingered inside her, stirring faint echoes of those moments, and she found herself unable to push the memories away.

Reluctantly, she spoke, her voice trembling. "You want me to… think about the kisses? Why does that matter?"

Vashika's mischievous smile deepened, and she leaned in slightly, her tone soft and coaxing. "It matters, darling, because this is about confronting the spell fully. Understanding its hold on you. You must embrace those moments, dissect them, and decide which one truly resonated with you. Only then can you take control."

Nisha hesitated, her stomach churning with unease. But she knew there was no escaping this. Slowly, she began to speak, her voice barely above a whisper.

Clara.

Her mind first turned to Clara, the stranger at the bus stop. The memory of Clara's kiss came rushing back—unexpected, overpowering, and filled with raw intensity. "Clara was… strong," Nisha admitted reluctantly, her voice shaking. "The kiss was overwhelming. It wasn't gentle, but it was passionate in a way that scared me. She was so… certain, so sure of what she wanted. I couldn't stop her."

She paused, her face flushing as the spell stirred faint feelings she didn't want to acknowledge. "It was bold," she added, her voice soft. "And part of me… admired that, I guess. But it also felt so… chaotic."

Shaya.

Her voice wavered as she spoke about Shaya, the memory sharper and more painful. "Shaya was… confident. Almost domineering. When she kissed me, it was like she wasn't just kissing me—she was claiming me." Her tears welled up as she admitted, "I didn't realize it at the time, but I helped her. I said things I didn't mean, but… in the moment, they felt real. She made me feel trapped, but also… seen. For the first time, I wasn't invisible to her."

The words left a bitter taste in her mouth, and she shook her head. "It was the most confusing feeling. I hated it, but part of me…" She trailed off, unable to finish the thought.

Elma.

The sweeper's kiss was next, and the memory sent a shiver down Nisha's spine. "Elma was… different," she said, her voice hesitant. "She was gentle at first, almost… reverent. But there was something about her. She was experienced, like she knew exactly what she was doing." Nisha's cheeks flushed as she recalled the moment she had handed the cardigan back, her actions blurred by the spell's influence.
"She… she made me feel like I wasn't in control at all," Nisha admitted, her voice trembling.

"But her kiss was… deliberate. It wasn't rushed or frantic. It was almost… careful. And that made it scarier."

Aasha.

Finally, her thoughts turned to Aasha, the nun in the church. The sacred setting made the memory feel surreal and wrong, but it was vivid nonetheless. "Aasha's kiss was… intense," she whispered, her voice barely audible. "She wasn't like the others. She had this calmness about her, even as the spell took hold. It was like… she was convincing me it was okay, even when I knew it wasn't."

Her face burned as she admitted, "I… I gave in completely. I said things I shouldn't have. I wanted it, even though I didn't understand why." Her voice broke as she finished, "It felt the most real, like she wasn't just taking—she was giving, too."

Vashika clapped her hands together softly, her smile sly and knowing. "Good, darling," she said smoothly. "You've done well to reflect on those moments. Now tell me—" She leaned closer, her voice dropping to a sultry whisper. "Which one was the best? Which one left the deepest mark on you?"

Nisha's heart raced, her cheeks flushing as she struggled to answer, her mind clouded with conflicting emotions.
What do you do next?

Nisha's cheeks flushed deeply as she stood there, her breath hitching slightly. The memories of the day's encounters flooded her mind, not just with fear and confusion, but with a strange, undeniable pull. As she reflected on each kiss, something shifted inside her—a part of her that the spell had awakened, stirring feelings she couldn't entirely suppress.
Her thoughts lingered on Shaya, and despite everything, a warmth spread through her chest. The kiss with her sister, though it had been forced, now felt vivid and charged in her mind.

She swallowed hard, her voice trembling as she finally spoke. "Shaya," she said softly, her eyes darting away from Vashika's intense gaze. "The kiss with Shaya was… the best."

Vashika smiled wider, her expression smug and triumphant, but she said nothing, waiting for Nisha to continue.

Nisha hesitated, her words catching in her throat before spilling out. "It wasn't just the kiss," she admitted, her voice low. "It was… everything. The way she pushed me against the wall, how her hands were so confident, so sure of what she wanted. She didn't hesitate, didn't ask—she just took what she wanted."

She bit her lip, her cheeks burning as she continued, her voice thick with emotion. "At first, I fought back. I tried to resist. But then… something changed. I stopped fighting. I… I gave in." Her breath quickened as the memories became more vivid. "I helped her take my top off. I said things I didn't mean—or maybe I did in that moment. I told her I wanted her more than anyone. And… it felt true, even if I didn't understand why."

Nisha's hands trembled as she covered her face, trying to steady herself. "There was something about it. The way she made me feel so… exposed. Vulnerable. But also… seen. Like I wasn't just invisible to her anymore. Like, for the first time, I mattered to her, even if it was twisted and wrong."

She looked up at Vashika, her eyes wide and conflicted. "That kiss… it wasn't just a kiss. It was… everything I've never felt before. Passion. Power. Desire. And I… I can't stop thinking about it."

Vashika's smile grew wider, her dark eyes glittering with satisfaction. She stepped closer, her voice a low, sultry purr. "Ah, my darling," she said, her tone dripping with amusement and intrigue. "Now you're beginning to understand. The spell hasn't just touched them—it's touched you. It's awakening something inside you. Something you've buried for too long."
Nisha's heart raced as she stared at Vashika, her mind a chaotic mess of emotions. She couldn't deny what she was feeling, no matter how much it terrified her. The spell wasn't just ruining her life—it was changing her, pulling her into a world she didn't recognize.

Nisha's eyes widened as Vashika stepped closer, her presence magnetic and commanding. Vashika ' lips curved into a knowing, mischievous smile, her gaze locking onto Nisha's with an intensity that made the younger girl's breath catch.

"Use the same intensity," Vashika said softly, her voice dripping with seduction. "Take all that passion, all that longing you felt with Shaya, and direct it at me. Go all in on me, Nisha. Let yourself go completely. That's the only way to break the spell."

Nisha blinked, her heart pounding as her body tensed with a mix of fear and hesitation. "Go all in?" she repeated, her voice shaky. "What are you talking about? How will that…?"

Vashika tilted her head, her dark hair cascading over one shoulder. Her smile deepened, sly and full of mystery. "Darling, the spell is tied to your inhibitions, your resistance," she explained, her tone smooth and hypnotic. "The only way to burn it out completely is to surrender to it entirely. Let it consume you, just as you let it consume Shaya, Clara, Elma, and Aasha." She leaned closer, her voice dropping to a whisper. "But this time, don't wait for it to take you. Take it yourself. Take me."

Nisha's stomach twisted, her thoughts swirling in confusion and doubt. "But… what if it doesn't work?" she asked, her voice barely audible.

Vashika's eyes glittered with something unreadable—anticipation, perhaps, or a deeper manipulation. "Oh, it will work," she said, her voice lilting. "Trust me, Nisha. Once you fully embrace the spell's power, it will release you. You'll break free from its hold. All you have to do is let go."

Nisha hesitated, her breaths shallow and quick as she stared at Vashika. The spell hummed inside her like a living thing, pulling at her, whispering to her. Part of her wanted to resist, to fight back—but another part, darker and more curious, felt the pull of Vashika's words, the temptation of surrender.

"Come closer," Vashika murmured, extending a hand. "Let me help you take the first step. Show me everything the spell has awakened in you."

Nisha's pulse quickened as she stood frozen, torn between fear and the strange, seductive allure of Vashika's offer. Was this the way to freedom—or was it another trap?

Nisha's breath was shallow as she stood frozen in the charged air of the room. Vashika's dark, enigmatic eyes seemed to pull her in, her voice like a siren's call echoing in her mind. Despite the fear twisting in her chest, something deeper—something the spell had awakened—pushed her forward.

Her body moved almost on its own, driven by the compulsion that now felt as much a part of her as her own heartbeat. Slowly, tentatively at first, she leaned forward, her lips parting slightly as she closed the gap between herself and Vashika.

Vashika's smile widened, her confidence unwavering as she waited, her presence radiating power and seduction. Nisha hesitated only a moment more before letting go of the last shred of resistance, surrendering to the pull of the spell.

Their lips met in a kiss that was unlike any Nisha had experienced that day. It wasn't forced or taken—it was deliberate, a passionate act of her own volition. Her hands moved instinctively to Vashika's face, her fingers tangling in the soft cascade of Vashika's dark hair as she deepened the kiss, her body pressing closer.

The air around them seemed to thrum with energy, the faint glow of the crystal ball flaring brighter as if reacting to their connection. Nisha kissed Vashika with an intensity she didn't know she possessed, her lips moving with a fervor that spoke of both desperation and surrender. For a moment, it was as if the spell itself was guiding her, fueling every touch, every movement, every flicker of emotion.

Vashika responded in kind, her arms wrapping around Nisha's waist, pulling her even closer. She kissed her back with a practiced, knowing passion, her movements confident and deliberate. It was as though she had expected this all along, had been waiting for this moment.

The room seemed to spin, the weight of the spell pressing down on Nisha even as she gave herself over to it. A strange warmth bloomed in her chest, spreading outward like fire, and for a fleeting second, she wondered if this was what freedom felt like—or if she was simply losing herself entirely.

When the kiss finally broke, Nisha gasped for air, her face flushed, her heart pounding. She stared at Vashika, her mind reeling with the intensity of what had just happened.

Nisha thought to herself, *"The kiss was electric, searing through me like lightning. It wasn't just a kiss—it was an unraveling, a surrender. And for a moment, I wasn't sure if I was breaking free or falling deeper into the spell's grasp."*

Vashika' smile was broader now, her eyes glinting with a triumphant light. She didn't say anything immediately, simply watching Nisha with that same enigmatic expression, as though waiting for her to realize the truth.

Vashika chuckled softly, her dark eyes gleaming with satisfaction. She tilted her head, a sly smile playing on her lips. "Nisha, you're just 18," she murmured, her voice dripping with playful amusement. "And yet… I had no idea you'd be such a good kisser. Where have you been hiding this talent, darling?"

Nisha, still breathless and flushed, felt her heart pounding in her chest. For a moment, her embarrassment mingled with a strange, heady confidence she couldn't entirely explain. She swallowed hard, her voice trembling as she responded, "Maybe... maybe I didn't know I had it in me." Her lips quirked into a hesitant smile, her eyes flickering with a mix of nervousness and boldness.

"But I guess..." Nisha continued, her voice growing steadier, "it's not just me, is it? Maybe you bring it out in people."

Vashika raised an eyebrow, clearly amused by the response. "Oh, Nisha," she purred, her voice low and teasing. "Perhaps I do. Or perhaps you've had it all along, waiting for someone to unlock it."

Nisha looked away for a moment, trying to steady her swirling emotions. "Well," she said softly, "if this is what it takes to break the spell, I guess I've learned something new about myself today."

Vashika's laughter was warm and rich, though the glint in her eyes remained sharp and knowing. "Oh, darling," she said, brushing a strand of hair from Nisha's face. "I think you've learned much more than that."

Vashika pulled back slightly, her hands still resting lightly on Nisha's shoulders as she gazed into her eyes with a soft, almost affectionate smile. "There, darling," she murmured, her voice smooth and reassuring. "It's done. The spell is broken."

Nisha blinked, her body still tingling from the intensity of their kiss. "It's... broken?" she asked hesitantly, her voice trembling with a mix of relief and lingering doubt.

Vashika nodded, her expression serene. "Yes," she said confidently, her lips curving into a gentle smile. "You confronted the spell, embraced it fully, and now it's gone. You're free, Nisha."

Nisha exhaled sharply, a weight lifting from her chest—or so she thought. She felt a flicker of hope, a desperate need to believe Vashika's words. "Really?" she asked, her voice barely above a whisper.
"Really," Vashika said warmly, her hands squeezing Nisha's shoulders lightly. "You've been through so much, and I know it wasn't easy. But you've done it. You've conquered it."

Nisha bit her lip, her eyes glistening with emotion. "I don't even know what to say," she admitted. "I hated you for putting me through all this, but… maybe you were just trying to help me all along. Maybe I… misjudged you."

Vashika chuckled softly, her dark eyes glimmering. "Perhaps you did," she said lightly. "But I hope this… intimate moment we've shared helps you see things differently. I never meant to harm you, darling. I only wanted to help you uncover your strength."

Nisha hesitated, her feelings a tangled mess of gratitude, lingering unease, and confusion. She searched Vashika ' face for any hint of deception but found only a calm, reassuring expression.

"Thank you," she said softly, her voice trembling. "I… I guess I forgive you."

Vashika's smile widened, and she brushed a hand lightly against Nisha's cheek. "Good," she said warmly. "That's all I wanted."

But deep inside, the spell remained—its influence still lurking, still coiling through

Nisha's thoughts and emotions. Unbeknownst to her, the ordeal was far from over.

As Nisha prepared to leave, still trying to process everything, Vashika leaned casually against the doorway, her dark eyes watching her intently. Her lips curved into a knowing smile, and she tilted her head slightly, her tone smooth and teasing.

"Before you go, darling," Vashika said, her voice laced with curiosity and mischief, "I have one last question for you."

Nisha stopped, glancing back at her with a mix of uncertainty and exhaustion. "What is it?" she asked cautiously.

Vashika stepped closer, her smile deepening. "When you first came to me, you were so consumed with the idea of catching that boy's attention. So desperate for his affection." Her eyes glinted with intrigue as she studied Nisha's expression. "But after everything you've been through today... after all those moments, those *connections*..."

She paused, letting the weight of her words linger in the air before finishing with a low, seductive lilt. "Tell me, Nisha—do you still long for that boy's attention? Or has today… changed your feelings? Made you more intimate toward women, perhaps?"
Nisha's breath hitched, her mind racing. The question felt like a trap, stirring something inside her that she wasn't ready to confront. She hesitated, biting her lip as her cheeks flushed.

"I…" she started, her voice trembling. She didn't know how to answer. The feelings she'd experienced throughout the day, the confusing emotions, the lingering sensations of the kisses—they all swirled together, making her question what she truly wanted.

Vashika stepped closer, her voice soft and coaxing. "Be honest with yourself, darling. The truth isn't something to fear. It's something to embrace."

Nisha's heart pounded as she tried to find the words, her mind torn between the person she thought she was and the feelings she couldn't ignore.

Nisha's lips parted slightly as she struggled to form an answer, her thoughts a tangled web of emotions she couldn't fully unravel. Her voice trembled when she finally spoke, her words halting and unsure.

"I… I don't know," she admitted, her cheeks flushing deeply. "All my life, I've only ever thought about guys. I've dreamed of falling for someone, of them liking me back. It was always about… him. That one boy. That's what I wanted. That's what I came to you for."

She paused, glancing down at her hands as if searching for clarity in her own words. "But now… after everything today…" Her voice faltered, and she looked up, her eyes glistening with confusion. "It's like… I don't even know myself anymore. What I felt today—what I experienced—it wasn't anything I ever expected. It wasn't anything I thought I could ever feel."

Vashika's smile widened slightly, her dark eyes sparkling with interest as she leaned closer. "Go on," she encouraged softly. "You're discovering something about yourself, darling. Don't stop now."

Nisha hesitated, her breath catching as her emotions bubbled to the surface. "When I think about the things that happened today, it's... confusing," she admitted. "Because even though I was scared, even though I hated what the spell did to me, there were moments..." Her voice grew quieter, almost a whisper. "Moments where I felt something. Something I didn't understand, something I didn't want to feel—but I did."

She looked up at Vashika, her expression both pleading and conflicted. "And now I don't know what's real. I don't know if it's the spell, or if it's... me. I don't know who I am anymore."
Vashika's gaze softened, her smile turning gentle but still tinged with mischief. "Ah, darling," she murmured, her voice like velvet. "You're standing at a crossroads, and it's perfectly natural to feel lost. But perhaps the question isn't whether the spell changed you. Perhaps the real question is..."

She leaned in, her voice dropping to a near whisper. "What do you *want* now?"

Nisha swallowed hard, her pulse quickening. The question hung in the air, pulling at her thoughts, her feelings, her very sense of self. She had no easy answer.

Nisha took a deep breath, her voice steady but quiet as she looked at Vashika. "I don't know what I want yet," she admitted, her words deliberate. "But I'll find out. Gradually. On my own terms."

Vashika's lips curled into a soft, knowing smile, her eyes gleaming with a hint of mischief (knowing that she will ofcourse find out but on her terms or under the control of Vashika that needs to be seen).

"Of course, darling," she replied smoothly, stepping back toward the shadows of her cottage. "Take all the time you need. The answers will come to you… eventually."

Nisha turned, her mind still spinning with the events of the day, and walked away from the cottage. She didn't look back, but she could feel Vashika's gaze lingering on her, heavy with secrets and amusement.

Vashika watched Nisha disappear into the distance, her smile deepening. Oh, Nisha, she thought to herself, a sly chuckle escaping her lips. *The spell is far from broken. You've only just begun to discover its reach.*

Chapter – 8 Home Sweet Home

The walk home was quiet, the streets eerily empty under the dim glow of the streetlights. Nisha's mind raced, replaying the surreal moments of the day and the lingering weight of the spell. Despite what Vashika had said, a part of her couldn't shake the feeling that something still lingered, coiled around her like a shadow she couldn't escape.

When she finally reached her house, her heart sank at the thought of Shaya. What would she find? Would Shaya remember what had happened between them? Would the spell's influence have faded, leaving her sister with no memory of the day's events? Or… would Shaya remember *everything*?

Her hands trembled slightly as she knocked on the door. The house was silent for a moment before she heard footsteps approaching from within. Her chest tightened, her thoughts a storm of uncertainty and fear.

As the door opened, Nisha braced herself for what—or who—she might face.

As the door creaked open, Nisha's heart sank in surprise when she saw her mother standing there instead of Shaya. Her mother, a poised woman in her early 40s with a warm but often stern demeanor, was dressed casually in a cardigan and jeans, her face etched with concern.

"Mom?" Nisha asked, her voice laced with confusion. "What are you doing here?"

Her mother stepped aside, gesturing for Nisha to come in. "I got a call from Shaya," she explained, her tone tinged with worry. "She said she wasn't feeling well, so I came over to check on her. I didn't expect to see you out so late, though. Where have you been?"

Nisha hesitated, trying to mask the storm of emotions from the day. "I was just… out," she replied vaguely. "How is she?"

Her mother closed the door behind her and led Nisha toward the living room, where Shaya lay sprawled on the couch, unconscious but breathing steadily. A blanket was draped over her, and the faint glow of the table lamp illuminated her pale face.

"She's been like this since I arrived," her mother said, kneeling beside Shaya and brushing a strand of hair from her face. "Do you know what happened to her, Nisha? Was she sick earlier, or…?"
Nisha's stomach twisted as she looked at Shaya, the memories of the day flooding back in vivid detail. She forced herself to remain calm, shaking her head as she replied, "I… I have no idea. She seemed fine earlier."

Her mother's gaze lingered on Nisha for a moment, her eyes narrowing slightly as though she were searching for answers. Then, with a sigh, she stood and walked toward the kitchen. "Well, I'll keep an eye on her tonight," she said. "If she doesn't wake up soon, I might take her to the hospital. You should get some rest."

Nisha nodded, glancing once more at Shaya before turning toward the stairs. As she moved, her mother's eyes lingered on her, something in her expression softening and shifting. Nisha didn't notice the way her mother's gaze trailed her movements, her concern for Shaya beginning to wane as an odd, growing focus on Nisha took hold.

Upstairs in her room, Nisha closed the door behind her, leaning against it with a sigh of relief. She hadn't expected to see her mother, and the sight of Shaya unconscious had rattled her more than she wanted to admit.

At least the spell is broken, she thought to herself, Vashika's reassurances echoing in her mind. She shook her head, trying to push away the lingering doubts. *Everything will be fine now. I just need to move on.*

Downstairs, however, her mother stood in the hallway, her thoughts clouded by something unfamiliar. Her gaze flickered back to the stairs where Nisha had disappeared, her concern for Shaya slipping further from her mind.
"Nisha," she murmured softly to herself, a strange warmth blooming in her chest. "She's… changed."

The spell, though hidden, still lingered in the air, weaving its insidious influence, unnoticed by Nisha but quietly taking hold of her mother.

Nisha was sitting on her bed, her knees pulled up to her chest as she stared out of her window, trying to make sense of the whirlwind day. The soft knock on her door startled her.

"Come in," she called, her voice weary but steady.

Her mother stepped into the room, carrying a faint smile and an air of warmth. She closed the door behind her gently, the dim glow of the bedside lamp casting a soft light on her face.

"Hey, sweetheart," her mother said, her tone casual but laced with a certain tenderness. "I thought I'd check on you. It's been such a strange day with Shaya and everything… and I realized we haven't really had much time to talk lately."

Nisha blinked, her brow furrowing slightly. "Talk? About what?"

Her mother crossed the room and sat down at the edge of the bed, smoothing her hands over her jeans. She glanced at Nisha with a gentle smile, her eyes lingering a moment longer than usual. "About anything. About you. I feel like I don't know much about my own daughter anymore," she said softly.

Nisha felt a pang of guilt, her defenses lowering as she looked at her mother. "What do you mean? You know me better than anyone," she said, her voice quiet.

Her mother reached out, resting a hand on Nisha's knee in a comforting gesture. "I used to think that," she said, her tone warm and wistful. "But as you've grown older, I feel like I've missed out on so much. You've become such a beautiful, strong young woman, and I just… I don't know. I want us to be closer. To really solidify the bond we have as mother and daughter."

Nisha's heart swelled with emotion at her mother's words. She felt a lump rise in her throat as she looked at the woman who had always been her rock, her foundation. "Mom," she said softly, her voice trembling slightly, "that means so much to me. I… I guess I've been so caught up in my own stuff that I didn't realize you felt that way."

Her mother's smile widened, a subtle warmth in her gaze. "You're my daughter, Nisha. No matter how busy life gets, no matter what happens, you'll always be the most important thing to me."

Nisha felt her eyes well up, a tear slipping down her cheek. She reached out, taking her mother's hand in hers. "I love you, Mom," she said, her voice breaking with emotion.
Her mother squeezed her hand gently, her touch lingering a moment longer than Nisha expected. "And I love you, sweetheart," she said, her voice soft and soothing.

Nisha felt her guard drop completely as the moment stretched, feeling closer to her mother than she had in a long time. Unbeknownst to her, the spell's influence subtly wove itself deeper into the atmosphere, pulling her mother's attention away from everything else, focusing entirely on Nisha.

Nisha's mother gently stroked her hand, her voice becoming softer, more tender, as she spoke. "You know, Nisha, when you were little, I used to sit by your bed every night after you fell asleep. I'd watch you breathe, so peaceful and innocent, and I'd think to myself, *how did I get so lucky to have a daughter like you?*"

Nisha's heart ached at the words, her emotions swelling as she listened. She could see the sincerity in her mother's eyes, or at least what she believed was sincerity.

"I was so scared of failing you," her mother continued, her tone growing wistful. "Of not being the kind of mother you needed. And as you grew up, I started to feel like you were slipping away from me, like I wasn't as close to you as I used to be. You have your own life now, your own thoughts and dreams, and I just..." She paused, her voice trembling slightly. "I miss the days when I was your everything."

Nisha felt tears welling up again, her mother's words striking a deep chord within her. "Mom, you'll always be important to me," she said, her voice breaking. "I know I've been distant, but it's not because I don't love you. I do. I just..." She trailed off, struggling to find the right words.

Her mother leaned in slightly, her gaze soft but intense. "I know, sweetheart," she said soothingly. "I just want to make sure you always feel how much you mean to me. That no matter what happens in life, you'll always know that I'm here for you. That I'll always be your biggest supporter, your greatest admirer."

Nisha's tears spilled over as she nodded, overcome by the flood of emotions. Her mother's words wrapped around her like a warm blanket, comforting and reassuring.
"You're everything to me, Nisha," her mother said, her voice dropping to a near whisper. "You're so special, so beautiful, inside and out. I just… I want us to be as close as we can be. Nothing else matters more to me than that."

Her mother leaned forward, opening her arms. "Come here, sweetheart," she murmured, her voice soft and inviting. "Let me hold you, like I used to when you were little."

Nisha didn't hesitate. Overcome with emotion, she leaned into her mother's embrace, wrapping her arms tightly around her. Her mother's warmth and familiar scent made her feel safe, loved, and connected in a way she hadn't felt in a long time.

Her mother's arms tightened around her, holding her firmly yet tenderly. The hug lingered, a closeness that felt deeper and more intense than usual. Nisha let herself melt into it, unaware of the subtle shift in her mother's demeanor, the way the spell quietly deepened its hold.

As Nisha's mother pulled back from the embrace, her hands lingered on Nisha's shoulders, her eyes studying her daughter's face with an intensity that felt almost unnerving. "Nisha," the mother murmured softly, her voice trembling slightly, "I wish I could take away all the struggles you've been through today. I just want to make you feel safe. Loved. Like you don't have to carry any of it alone."

Nisha, exhausted from the day's emotional and physical toll, let her eyes flutter closed. "Thanks, Mom," she whispered, her voice heavy with weariness. "I don't know what I'd do without you."

But as she rested, her defenses lowered, something shifted in the room. The spell, lurking quietly, sprang into full force, its insidious influence wrapping around Velvet's thoughts like a serpent. Her tender, motherly concern twisted into something obsessive, something unrecognizable, as the spell rewrote her feelings, amplifying them into an uncontrollable longing.

Nisha Mother's gaze darkened, her breathing quickening as her hands moved instinctively to brush Nisha's hair back from her face. Her touch lingered, her fingers trailing down Nisha's cheek, and her lips parted as she whispered, "Nisha… you're so beautiful."

Nisha, her eyes still closed, smiled faintly at the words, thinking them nothing more than motherly affection. But when mother's hands moved, one brushing against her collarbone and the other trailing lightly down her arm, Nisha's brow furrowed. She opened her eyes, confusion flashing across her face.

"Mom?" she asked hesitantly, shifting slightly under her mother's touch.
Nisha's mother didn't answer right away. Her eyes, clouded with the spell's influence, were fixed on Nisha's face, her expression filled with an unsettling mix of tenderness and longing.

"You're everything to me," She [mother] murmured, her voice low and trembling. "I don't think I've ever realized how much… until now."

Nisha's chest tightened as unease began to creep into her. She tried to move back, but her mother's hands tightened slightly on her shoulders, holding her in place. "Mom, what are you doing?" she asked, her voice rising with panic.

Mother leaned in closer, her face inches from Nisha's, her breath warm against her skin. "Shh, it's okay, sweetheart," she said softly, her tone soothing yet unnervingly intense. "You've been through so much today. Let me take care of you. Let me… make you feel better."
Nisha's heart pounded as alarm bells went off in her mind. "No, Mom, stop—" she began, but she [mother] silenced her with a finger pressed gently to her lips.

"You don't have to be afraid," she [mother] murmured, her voice dripping with an almost hypnotic reassurance. Her hands moved with increasing confidence, trailing over Nisha's arms and shoulders as her gaze remained locked on her daughter's.

Panic surged in Nisha as the weight of the spell's influence became undeniable. "Mom, this isn't you!" she cried, trying to pull away. "It's the spell! You're not thinking clearly—please, stop!"

But she [mother] was too far gone, the spell's grip twisting her maternal love into something obsessive and overpowering. She leaned in, her lips brushing against Nisha's forehead, then her cheek, as her hands moved to hold Nisha in place.

The room felt suffocating, the air thick with the spell's dark energy as Velvet's actions mirrored those of Clara, Shaya, Elma, and Aasha before her. Nisha's mind raced, torn between shock, fear, and a creeping sense of helplessness as she realized the nightmare wasn't over.

Nisha's heart raced as she looked into Velvet's eyes, searching for a sign of recognition, of the motherly care she knew and trusted. But the spell's lingering influence had taken hold, twisting and distorting the relationship into something unrecognizable. Panic surged within her, and she quickly wriggled free from Velvet's grip, her mind racing for a way to break through the haze.

"Mom!" Nisha said firmly, stepping back and holding up her hands. "You're not acting like yourself. This isn't you—it's the spell. You have to fight it."

She [mother] blinked, confusion flickering across her face as if she were caught in a battle between her real self and the spell's pull. She took a step forward, but Nisha held her ground, her voice trembling but determined.

"I know you love me," Nisha continued, trying to reach the real mother beneath the spell's haze. "But this isn't love. This is something else, something wrong. Please… please listen to me. You have to stop."

The tension in the room was palpable, the spell's energy still thick and oppressive, but she [mother] hesitated. Her gaze softened for a brief moment, as if her true self was struggling to break free. She reached out, her hand trembling, but this time it stopped short of touching Nisha.

"I…" the mother whispered, her voice faltering. She closed her eyes tightly, her breathing uneven as she seemed to wrestle with the conflicting emotions and compulsions within her.

Nisha took a step closer, her voice softening. "You're stronger than this. You've always been strong for me, and I need you to be strong now. Please, fight it."

The mother staggered slightly, clutching her head as though the spell's influence was causing her physical pain. Nisha didn't dare move closer, unsure of whether her real mother or the spell would respond.

After a long, agonizing moment, the mother sank to her knees, tears streaming down her face. "I don't know what's happening to me," she whispered, her voice broken. "It's like I can't control it… but I don't want to hurt you. Nisha, I don't want to hurt you."

Nisha felt a wave of relief mingled with sadness as she knelt beside her mother, her heart aching for the woman she had always looked up to. "You're not going to hurt me," she said softly, placing a reassuring hand on Velvet's shoulder. "We're going to figure this out. Together."

The spell's hold still loomed like a shadow over them, but for the moment, the real mother seemed to be fighting her way back. She took her mother to another room and placed her on a comfortable bed and asked her to sleep. She locked the door from outside.

Back in her room, Nisha sat on the floor of her room, trembling, her back pressed against the door she had just locked. Her heart raced, and her thoughts spiraled out of control. She couldn't stop replaying the events of the day—the kisses, the spell's manipulations, and now, the horrifying distortion of her mother's love. It was as if every safe space in her life had been invaded, corrupted by a force she didn't fully understand.

Her hands balled into fists, her nails digging into her palms as anger bubbled to the surface. **"This isn't my life,"** she whispered through clenched teeth, her voice trembling with a mix of fury and desperation. **"This isn't who I am, and I won't let it control me."**

But the truth was, she didn't know how to stop it. The spell was like a poison coursing through her life, warping everything it touched—and now, it wasn't just about the people it affected. It was about her. Her thoughts. Her actions. Her identity. She stared at her reflection in the darkened window, her tear-streaked face staring back at her like a stranger.

"Vashika," she muttered, the name tasting bitter on her tongue. A fresh wave of anger surged through her as she stood, her legs shaky but determined. **"She did this to me. She promised me power, promised me something special, and instead, she's turned my world into a nightmare."**

Nisha paced the room, her mind racing. She couldn't go back to her mother, couldn't face Shaya or anyone else in her life until she understood the full extent of the spell and found a way to break it for good. But confronting Vashika meant more than seeking answers—it meant demanding justice. And it meant accepting the possibility that the answers she found might be darker than she was prepared for.

Her breath hitched as a chilling thought crept into her mind: **What if there was no way out? What if Vashika had bound her to this curse forever?**

She clenched her fists, her jaw tightening. **"No,"** she said aloud, her voice firmer this time. **"I'm not her pawn. I'm not anyone's pawn. I'll find a way to end this—even if it means confronting the very darkness she claims I have to embrace."**

A flicker of resolve sparked in her chest, though it was dim and fragile against the overwhelming weight of her situation. Nisha grabbed her phone and glanced at the clock. The night was far from over, and she knew exactly where she had to go.

"Vashika," she whispered, her voice steady now, her anger a blazing fire in her chest. **"You started this, and I'm going to make sure you finish it."**

As she stepped out into the night, the air felt heavier, as though the very universe knew what lay ahead. Her mind churned with questions she would demand answers to—and with the determination to either reclaim her life or burn down whatever sinister web Vashika had trapped her in. But one thing was clear: this wasn't over.

It was only the beginning.

Teaser For 'Manipulation - Part-2'

"Nisha thought the nightmare was over. But the spell's remnants lingered in ways she hadn't imagined, and Vashika's secrets were far from fully revealed.

As new faces enter her life and old ones return, the stakes only grow higher in her quest for freedom.

Will Nisha finally break free, or will she fall even deeper into the web of manipulation? Find out in the upcoming *'Part 2: The Seductive Trap of Vashika'*

About the Author

Arjun Pitcher is a storyteller who weaves tales that blend the mystical with the profoundly human, exploring the complexities of relationships, identity, lust, seduction, bound and desire. Born with an unquenchable curiosity for the extraordinary desires hidden within the ordinary, Arjun Pitcher began writing weaving stories at a young age, captivated by the magic of words and their power to transport readers to worlds both enchanting and unsettling.

Manipulation: The Curse of Kisses marks a bold foray into the intricate interplay of emotion and supernatural influence, showcasing Arjun's talent for creating deeply flawed yet compelling characters. Through Nisha's journey, Arjun invites readers to question the nature of control, consent, and the hidden depths of human longing.

When not writing, Arjun can be found delving into movies, exploring the psychology of relationships, or simply enjoying quiet moments with a cup of tea and a notebook in hand. Passionate about storytelling that challenges and resonates, Arjun (under the brand of **Pen N Plot Productions**) continues to create narratives that leave a lasting impression, offering readers both escape and reflection. This is the 3rd book written by Arjun Pitcher. His previous two offering are mentioned on the next page.

1. The Secret Seller (2024)
2. Manipulation: The Curse of Kisses (2024)
3. Main BETA (β) Hu!: Stuck in Time-Loop (2024)
4. Enchantress of Chandrakanta Fort (2025)

Connect with Arjun Pitcher on Instagram - **pennplot_production** and stay tuned for the highly anticipated continuation of Nisha's story in the sequel.

Dear Readers,

Thank you for joining me on this captivating journey through the mysteries and allure of **Manipulation: The Curse of Kisses**. Your support means the world to me, and I hope the story resonated with you, stirred your imagination, and left you wanting more.

If you enjoyed the book—or even if you have suggestions for improvement—I would be immensely grateful if you could take a moment to leave a review on the website. Your thoughts not only help me grow as a writer but also guide other readers who might be intrigued by the tale of Nisha.

Every review, whether a few words or a detailed reflection, makes a difference. Your voice helps this story reach more hearts and minds. Thank you for your time, your feedback, and for being part of this enchanting adventure.

With gratitude,
Arjun Pitcher

THANK YOU SO MUCH FOR READING THIS BOOK !!